ANTOINE DE SAINT-EXUPERY

Southern Mail *and* Night Flight

*

TRANSLATED FROM THE FRENCH BY

CURTIS CATE

(with acknowledgements to Stuart Gilbert's translations)

PENGUIN BOOKS

PENGUIN BOOKS

Published by the Penguin Group
Penguin Books Ltd, 27 Wrights Lane, London W8 5TZ, England
Penguin Putnam Inc., 375 Hudson Street, New York, New York 10014, USA
Penguin Books Australia Ltd, Ringwood, Victoria, Australia
Penguin Books Canada Ltd, 10 Alcorn Avenue, Toronto, Ontario, Canada M4V 3B2
Penguin Books (NZ) Ltd, Private Bag 102902, NSMC, Auckland, New Zealand

Penguin Books Ltd, Registered Offices: Harmondsworth, Middlesex, England

Courrier Sud first published by Gallimard 1929
First English translation (*Southern Mail*) translated by Stuart Gilbert,
published in the USA by Harrison Smith & Robert Haas, 1933
This revised translation by Curtis Cate first published by William Heinemann Ltd 1971
Published in Penguin Books 1976
Vol de Nuit first published by Gallimard 1931
First English translation (*Night Flight*), translated by Stuart Gilbert,
published by Crosby Continental Editions 1932
Published in Penguin Books 1939
This revised translation by Curtis Cate first published by William Heinemann Ltd 1971
Published in Penguin Books 1976
Reprinted in Penguin Classics 2000
1

Courrier Sud copyright 1929 by Éditions Gallimard
Vol de Nuit copyright 1931 by Éditions Gallimard
Southern Mail and *Night Flight*
Reissued translations copyright © William Heinemann Ltd, 1971
All rights reserved

Printed in Great Britain by Antony Rowe Ltd, Chippenham, Wiltshire
Set in Linotype Granjon

Except in the United States of America, this book is sold subject
to the condition that it shall not, by way of trade or otherwise, be lent,
re-sold, hired out, or otherwise circulated without the publisher's
prior consent in any form of binding or cover other than that in
which it is published and without a similar condition including this
condition being imposed on the subsequent purchaser

Contents

Translator's Preface 7
SOUTHERN MAIL 9
Preface by André Gide 105
NIGHT FLIGHT 109

Translator's Preface

Several years ago, at a time when I was engaged in writing a biography of Saint-Exupéry, I called on Stuart Gilbert, intrigued to know how it was that he had been selected to translate *Vol de Nuit* and, a little later, *Courrier Sud*. The story of just how this came about is too long to be told here, but briefly speaking, it involved three remarkable expatriates – Sylvia Beach, James Joyce, and Caresse Crosby, in that order. Generous as ever, Joyce even gave him the benefit of his thick-lensed advice, though that did not keep Gilbert from remarking to me somewhat wistfully towards the end of his narrative: 'If I were translating it today' – he was speaking of *Courrier Sud* – 'I would be much severer with myself.'

Little did I realize, in garnering this characteristically modest reminiscence, that less than one year later Stuart Gilbert would be dead; still less that at the request of Saint-Exupéry's British publishers, I should be asked to attempt what he had no longer had the time or the energy to undertake. How he would have gone about it I have no idea; but I feel reasonably sure that in the process some of the baroque lyricism would have gone. To prune *Southern Mail* of all of it is, of course, impossible; for the tone of lyrical despair – strongly influenced by Jean Giraudoux's novelistic style as well as by Nietzsche, Proust, and Bergson's philosophizings on duration, identity, and time – is very marked in the original.

If it is less obvious in *Night Flight*, it is simply because Saint-Exupéry, without ceasing to be a poet, was beginning to turn away from the 'romantic' – a term he came to abhor as synonymous with 'exaggerated' and 'overblown' – towards a less vaporous, more crystalline, in a word, towards a more classic style.

C.C.

Southern Mail

Part One

I

By radio. 6h.10. Toulouse to all airports: France–South America mail-plane left Toulouse 5h. 45 stop.

*

A sky as pure as water bathed the stars and brought them out. And then night fell. Dune by dune the Sahara unfolded itself beneath the moon. Its light, falling on our foreheads with the pallor of a lamp which blends the softened forms, enveloped every object in its velvet sheen. Under our soundless footsteps the sand had the richness of a carpet. And bare-headed we walked, freed of the cruel weight of the sun. In that dwelling place – the night . . .

Yet how could we trust this peacefulness? The trade winds flowed restlessly towards the south, rustling over the beach like silk. Unlike the winds of Europe, which shift and peter out, these pressed down on us as relentlessly as the airstream against a speeding train. Sometimes at night they hit us so hard that we would lean on them, our faces towards the north, with a feeling of being carried away, of pushing upstream against them towards some obscure goal. What haste, what disquiet!

The sun, continuing its course, brought back the daylight. The Moors were quiet. Those that ventured as far as the Spanish fort gesticulated and handled their guns like toys. This was the Sahara viewed from the wings of the stage: the untamed tribes were stripped of their mystery and became bit-part players.

Thus we lived opposite each other, victims of our own distorting images. And it was why in this desert we felt no isolation;

to appreciate the distance of our banishment we would have had to return home and to see it in perspective.

Captives of the Moors and of ourselves, we seldom ventured more than five hundred yards, there where the lawless wilderness began. Our nearest neighbours, at Cisneros and Port-Étienne, were five to six hundred miles away, also trapped by the Sahara, like flies in amber. We knew them by their surnames and their foibles, but between us there lay a silence as thick as interplanetary space.

This morning, however, the outside world sprang back to life, linked to us by two aerials planted in the sand. The radio operator handed us a morse message, announcing the weekly flight:

France–America mail-plane left Toulouse 5h. 45 stop passed Alicante 11h. 10.

Toulouse was speaking, the hub and headquarters, a distant god. In just ten minutes the news was broadcast to us via Barcelona, Casablanca, Agadir, only to be relayed on towards Dakar. Over a distance of three thousand miles all the airports were now alerted. At the pick-up hour of six o'clock, that evening, we received another message:

Mail-plane will land Agadir 21 hours leave for Cabo Juby 21h. 30 land there with Michelin flare stop Cabo Juby will prepare usual ground lights stop instructed maintain contact with Agadir. Signed: Toulouse.

From our observatory at Cape Juby, on the distant rim of the Sahara, we were tracking a distant comet.

The South now grew restive.

From Dakar to Port-Étienne, Cisneros, Juby: news of mail-plane urgently requested.

From Juby to Cisneros, Port-Étienne, Dakar: no news since passage Alicante 11h. 10.

Somewhere in the sky a plane droned. And from Toulouse as far as Senegal men strained their ears to hear it.

2

Toulouse. 5.30 a.m.

The airport car pulls up in front of the hangar, lying open to the windswept darkness. Its 500-candlepower bulbs light up its objects starkly, hard and brittle like those in a fun-fair booth. Beneath this ringing vault each spoken word lingers on, persists, charging the silence with its echoes.

With its gleaming metal hull and its carefully degreased engine, the plane looks new. A piece of intricate clockwork which the mechanics have fingered with the delicacy of inventors. Now they can step back from their handiwork.

'Step lively, there, step lively!'

Bag by bag the mail disappears into the belly of the plane. There is a rapid check: 'Buenos Aires ... Natal ... Dakar ... Casa ... Dakar ... Thirty-nine bags. Right?'

'Right.'

The pilot climbs into his togs. Several sweaters, a scarf, a leather flying suit, fur-lined boots. His still sleeping body feels heavy. Someone calls to him: 'Hey there, get a move on!' His hands encumbered with altimeter, watch, and map-holder, his fingers numb inside the thick gloves, he hoists himself awkwardly up to the cockpit. A deep-sea diver out of his element. But once settled into place, everything grows light.

A mechanic clambers up to speak to him.

'630 kilos.'

'Right. Any passengers?'

'Three.'

He takes charge of them without seeing them.

The airfield controller turns towards the ground-crew.

'Who cotter-pinned this cowling?'

'I did.'

'You're fined 20 francs.'

The airfield controller makes a final check. Everything in place, as in a ballet. This plane exactly as it should be in this hangar, as it will be in the sky five minutes hence. This missing cotter-pin – sticking out like a sore thumb. Those 500-watt bulbs, these piercing looks, this iron discipline all go to make this flight, relayed on from airfield to airfield as far as Buenos Aires or Santiago de Chile, a matter of ballistics rather than an affair of luck. So that storms, mists, tornados, the myriad vagaries of valve-springs, rocker-arms, and pistons notwithstanding, express trains, cargo-boats, and ocean liners will be outpaced, outdistanced, and left far behind! And Buenos Aires or Santiago reached in record time.

'Start her up!'

A slip of paper is handed up to Bernis, the pilot: his battle plan. He reads:

Perpignan reports clear sky, no wind. Barcelona, storm, Alicante...

*

Toulouse. 5.45 a.m.

The powerful wheels strain against the chocks. Flayed by the wind of the propeller, the grass for twenty yards behind seems to flow like a stream. With a movement of his wrist Bernis can unleash or curb the gale.

Now the sound swells, gunned into a dense, almost solid roar, into which the body is locked. When the pilot feels something unassuaged inside him now satisfied at last, he thinks 'that's fine'. Ahead of him the black cowling muzzles into the sky like a howitzer. Beyond the propeller the dawn landscape trembles.

Taxi-ing slowly into the wind, he pulls the throttle-lever towards him. Hooked by the propeller, the plane leaps forward. The first bumps on the elastic air are cushioned, and now at last the taut ground seems to stretch and gleam beneath his wheels like a transmission belt. Having gauged the air – at first impalpable, then fluid and now solid – the pilot bears down on it and rises.

The trees bordering the landing field uncover the horizon as they slip from sight. From six hundred feet up it is still an inhabited earth one gazes down upon – toy sheepfolds with painted houses and trees standing extraordinarily erect, and woods that shield their furry thickness.

Bernis seeks the proper angle for his back, the exact position of his elbow best suited to his ease. Behind him the low clouds smudge Toulouse like railway station roofs. Gradually he relaxes his grip on the plane, which seeks to rise, giving freer play to the force his hand contains. With a movement of his wrist he frees each swell which lifts him up and surges through him like a wave.

In five hours Alicante, and at sundown Africa. A mood of calm comes over him and Bernis begins to dream. 'I've cleared things up.' Yesterday he had left Paris by the night express, but what a strange holiday it had been! The dim recollection he has of it is of some sombre uproar. Later he would suffer, but for the moment he has left everything behind, to continue on without him. For the present he feels himself being reborn with the rising dawn and contributing to build another day. 'I am only a workman, delivering the African mail,' he thinks. 'Each day, for the workman who begins to build a world, the world begins.'

'I've cleared things up...' He recalled that last evening in the apartment – newspapers wrapped round piles of books. Letters burned or filed away, the furniture draped in sheets. Each object isolated, dragged from its ambit, relocated. And this tumult of the heart which no longer made sense.

He had prepared himself for the next day as for a journey. He had embarked on the morrow as though for an America. But so many unfinished things still bound him to himself. Then suddenly he was free. Bernis was almost frightened to find himself so dispensable, so mortal.

Beneath him Carcassonne drifts past, with its emergency landing strip. What a well-ordered world, this too – ten thousand feet up – neatly laid out like a toy sheepfold in its box. Houses, canals, roads – men's playthings. A sectioned world, a chessboard world, where each field touches its fence, each park its wall. Carcassonne, where each milliner relives the life of her grandmother. Humble lives happily herded together, men's playthings neatly drawn up in their showcase. Yes, a showcase world, too exposed, to spread out, with towns laid out in order on the unrolled map and which a slow earth pulls towards him with the sureness of a tide.

'I'm alone,' he muses. The sunlight glances off his altimeter dial, an icy, luminous sun. A kick to the rudder-paddle and the entire landscape tilts. A steely light above a mineral earth: gone, abolished is all that makes for the softness, the scent, the frailty of living things. And yet, beneath this leather jacket, there is Bernis, a warm and ... oh so fragile ... flesh. Beneath those thick gloves are marvellous hands which knew, Geneviève, how to caress your face with the backs of their fingers.

But here is Spain.

3

Today, Jacques Bernis, you will cross Spain with the tranquillity of a proprietor. Familiar scenes will rise to meet you one by one. You will elbow your way with ease through the storms. Barcelona, Valencia, Gibraltar will sweep towards you and be borne away. As is fitting. You will discard your rolled up map and the work accomplished will pile up behind you. But I recall your first halting steps and the final words of advice I gave you prior to your first mail flight. At dawn you were due to take the meditation of people in your arms, in your weak arms, and carry them across a thousand pitfalls, like a treasure clutched beneath a cloak. The precious mail, they had told you, more precious than life. So fragile that a trifling mistake can send it up in flames and scatter it to the winds. I remember well that eve of battle.

'And then what?'

'You'll try to make the beach of Peñiscola. But watch out for the fishing-boats.'

'And then?'

'And then, from there as far as Valencia, you'll have no trouble finding emergency landing fields. I've underlined them here in red. If the worst comes to the worst, put down in one of the dry *ríos*.'

Beneath this green lamp-shade and in front of these outspread maps Bernis was back at school. But from each point on the ground his master today was extracting living secrets. Instead of dead figures, these unknown lands now yielded real fields and flowers – where there's a tree you must watch out for! – and real beaches with their sand where, in the gathering dusk, one must avoid the fishermen.

Already, Jacques Bernis, you realized that we would never know Granada nor Almería nor the mosques of the Alhambra, but only a stream or an orange orchard and the humblest of their secrets.

'Now listen – here if the weather's good, you can fly straight through. But if it's bad and you're flying low, veer left and follow this valley.'

'I follow this valley.'

'This pass will bring you back towards the sea.'

'I get back to the sea by this pass.'

'And watch out for your engine – among these cliffs and rocks.'

'But what if it stalls on me?'

'You squirm out of it somehow.'

Bernis smiled. Young pilots are romantics. A rock passes, like a sling-shot, and fells him. A child dashes by, but an outstretched arm strikes him on the forehead and bowls him over . . .

'But no, old boy, no – you hang on and scrape out of it as best you can.'

Bernis was proud of this new teaching. In his youth the *Aeneid* had failed to yield him a single secret capable of saving him from death. The teacher's finger poised over the map of Spain was no diviner's finger; it could reveal neither pitfall nor treasure, nor this shepherdess in her meadow.

What softness now radiated from this lamp! Its soft, yellow light was like the oil slick that becalms the sea. Outside it was windy. This room was an island in the midst of a stormy world, a seamen's inn.

'How about a glass of port?'

'Fine!'

Pilot's room, makeshift inn – how often we had to build it up again from scratch! The company would notify us in the evening: 'Pilot X is transferred to Senegal . . . to America . . .' That very night one would have to loose one's shore-lines, nail down one's crates, strip the room of one's photographs and books, and leave it less marked than by a ghost. Sometimes that same night, one had to unlock two clinging arms, exhaust the strength of a young girl – not reason with her (for they are all stubborn) but wear her down – and then towards three in the morning, deposit her in a gentle sleep, resigned, not to this departure, but to her grief, saying to oneself: 'She now accepts it – she's crying.'

What in your wanderings about the world, what in after-years, Jacques Bernis, did you learn? The plane? Slowly one advances, boring one's hole through solid crystal. Town gives way to town, and one must land to know aught of them. For these treasures are proffered only to be withdrawn, washed by the hours as by the sea. But – on coming back from these first flights, what sort of man did you think you had become? And why this yearning to confront him with the ghost of a tender-hearted kid? During your first leave you dragged me over to see our old boarding-school. From the Sahara, Bernis, where I await your arrival, I recall with melancholy this visit to our boyhood.

A white gabled house among the pines, one window lighting up and then another. And you said to me: 'Here is the study-hall where we wrote our first poems.'

We had come from afar. Our heavy cloaks quilted the world and our nomad souls kept watch in the centre of ourselves. We approached unknown cities with tight-set jaws, well protected and well gloved. The crowds flowed past without jostling us. Our white flannels and tennis shirts were reserved for the cities we had tamed – for Casablanca and Dakar. In Tangier we walked bare-headed, no armour being needed in this sleepy little town.

We came back stalwart, proud of our adult muscles. We had battled, we had suffered, we had crossed frontierless lands, we had loved a few women, occasionally played pitch and toss with death – all to rid ourselves of that youthful dread of punishments and detentions, all to be able to listen without flinching to the Saturday evening announcement of the weekly marks.

In the entrance-hall there was first a whispering, then voices calling, and finally a scurrying of aged feet. They came, draped in the golden lamplight, their cheeks like parchment but with shining eyes – of delight, of welcome! Instantly we understood that they knew us to be transformed: old boys habitually return with a firm step that claims its own revenge.

For neither my firm hand-shake nor the forthright gaze of Jacques Bernis surprised them. Without further ado they treated us like men, hurrying off to fetch a bottle of old Samos wine of which in the past they had never breathed a word.

We sat down for the evening meal. Beneath the shaded lamp they huddled like peasants around a hearth, and then it was we learned how weak they really were. Weak in their indulgence; for our erstwhile sloth – the sure road to moral wrack and ruin! –

they now chuckled over, as a childish failing. The pride they had once sought so strenuously to curb they now praised, terming it 'noble'.

Even the philosophy master made some strange admissions. Descartes had perhaps based his entire system on a *petitio principii*. Pascal ... Pascal was heartless. Strive as he might, he had been unable, before dying, to resolve the age-old problem of human liberty. He who had cautioned us so earnestly against determinism and Taine, he who could find no direr enemy for young boys coming out of school and into life than Nietzsche, now acknowledged some guilty predilections. Nietzsche ... even Nietzsche troubled him. And the reality of matter? He was no longer sure, it worried him. Whereupon they began to question us. We had sallied forth from this warm and sheltered house into the storms of life, and we must needs tell them what the weather was really like on earth. Whether a man who loves a woman becomes her slave, like Pyrrhus, or her executioner, like Nero; if Africa and its great wastes and its blue sky faithfully reflect the teaching of the geography master? (And what of the ostriches, who close their eyes in self-defence?) Jacques Bernis bowed his head; for though he harboured many secrets, his teachers kept prying them from him.

They wanted to hear him talk of the heady thrills of action, of the roar of his motor, to discover why to be happy, we could no longer content ourselves, like them, with the clipping of the rose-bushes in the evening. It was Bernis's turn to explain Lucretius or Ecclesiastes and to offer advice. He explained to them, while there was yet time, how much food and water one must take with one to keep from dying after crash-landing in the desert. Bernis threw them a few last scraps of advice – the secrets that can rescue a pilot from the Moors, the reflex actions which can save a pilot from burning up. They nodded, still rather anxious yet reassured and even proud to have unleashed such novel forces upon the world. At long last they could touch these heroes whom, from time immemorial, they had talked about, and having touched them, die. They spoke of Julius Caesar's boyhood.

But for fear of disheartening them, we also spoke to them of disappointments and the bitter taste that rest has after a useless action. And seeing the eldest of them lost in a reverie that pained us, we added that perhaps the only truth is the peace to be found in books. But this the teachers knew already. They knew of life's hardships, having had to teach history to others.

'But what brings you back to this part of the world?' Bernis gave no answer, but the old teachers, winking at each other out of their knowledge of the human heart, thought of love...

4

From up there the earth had looked bare and dead; but as the plane loses altitude, it robes itself in colours. The woods spread out their quilts, the hills and valleys rise and fall in waves, like someone breathing. A mountain over which he flies swells like some recumbent giant's breast, almost grazing his wing-tip.

Now close, like a torrent under a bridge, the earth begins its mad acceleration. The ordered world becomes a landslide, as houses and villages are torn from the smooth horizon and swept away behind him. The landing strip of Alicante rises, tilts, then steadies into place. The wheels graze and then grind into it as on a whet-stone.

As Bernis climbs out of the cockpit, his legs feel heavy. For a second he closes his eyes, his head still full of sky and the roar of his engine, his limbs still quivering from the vibrations of his machine. Then, entering the office, he slowly sits down, pushes aside the inkwell and several books, and pulls the flight plan for Plane 612 towards him.

Toulouse–Alicante: 5h. 15 flying time.

He pauses, yields to his weariness and his dreams. Vague sounds reach him – somewhere a woman is shouting. The driver of the Ford opens the door, apologizes, smiles. Bernis looks gravely at these walls, this door, and the driver – all of them life-size. For ten minutes he is involved in a discussion he doesn't understand, with the gestures forever rising, falling, rising. It all seems unreal. That tree, planted out there in front of the door, has been there for thirty years. For thirty years a witness.

Motor: nothing to report.
Plane: slight tilt to starboard.

He lays down the pen and thinks, 'I'm tired,' as the same vision hovers before his gaze. An amber light falling on a radiant landscape. Meadows and well-ploughed fields. A village off to the right, to the left a tiny flock of sheep, and covering them all the blue vault of heaven. 'A house,' thinks Bernis. He remembers having felt, with a sudden certitude, that this countryside, this sky, this earth were all built like a mansion. A well-ordered family mansion. Everything so vertical. No lurking danger, no flaw in the oneness of this vision, in the oneness of a landscape within which he is safely lodged.

Thus do old ladies feel eternal as they stand by the windows of their drawing-rooms. The lawn is fresh and green, the plodding gardener is watering the flowers. Their eyes follow his reassuring back. A delicious smell of wax rises from the polished floors. In the house all is as it should be, soft and gentle; the day has passed, trailing its wind and its sun and its showers and leaving the roses barely aged.

'Time to leave. Good-bye.' And Bernis takes off again.

He plunges into a storm, which batters at the plane like the pick-axe of a wrecker. He's been through others, he'll come through this one too. Bernis's thoughts are rudimentary, thoughts geared to action: how to climb out of this ring of mountains into which the whirling downdraughts are sucking him, how to see through this diluvial night and jump the black wall of whipping rain, and come out on to the sea?

A sudden shudder! Has something snapped? Suddenly the plane lurches towards the left. Bernis holds it back with one, then two hands, and then with every sinew of his body. 'God Almighty!' The plane drops earthwards like a weight. Bernis is done for. One more second and he'll be flung forever from that suddenly troubled mansion he was just beginning to understand. Fields, forests, villages will spiral up towards him. The smoke of appearances, wraiths of smoke, smoke! And here's a sheepfold doing somersaults across the sky . . .

'Whew! A nasty fright! . . .' A kick to the rudder-paddle frees a cable. A jammed control? Sabotage? No. Nothing. Nothing at all. A simple kick of the heel re-establishes the world. But what a close thing!

A close thing? All he can still feel of this second is a queer taste in the mouth, a sour sweat. Yes, and that suddenly-glimpsed flaw! So everything here was no more than make-believe – roads, canals, houses, all these playthings of mankind!

*

Over now and done with! Here the sky is clear. The weather forecast had announced it. 'Sky one quarter overcast with cirrus clouds.' Meteorology, isobars? Professor Björnson's 'cloud systems'? A radiant, national holiday sky. Yes, Bastille Day weather. 'It's fiesta day in Málaga,' is how they should have announced it. Each of its inhabitants the proud possessor of thirty thousand feet of pure sky above him. A sky rising clear to the cirrus clouds. Never was the aquarium so luminous, so vast. Like the afternoon of a regatta in the bay – with a blue sky, a blue sea, and a blue-eyed skipper in a blue sports-shirt collar. A holiday of light.

Over and done with. Thirty thousand letters come safely through. The airline company kept drilling it into you: the precious mail, more precious than life itself. Enough to keep thirty thousand lovers going ... Lovers, be patient! In the sinking fire of sunset here we come. Behind Bernis the clouds are thick, churned by the whirlwind in its mountain bowl. Before him lies a land decked out in sunlight, the tender muslin of the meadows, the rich tweed of the woods, the ruffled veil of the sea.

Night will fall as he overflies Gibraltar. A slow bank to the left – towards Tangier – will wrench Bernis from Europe, drifting off behind him like a gigantic ice-floe. A few more towns, nourished on brown earth, and then it will be Africa. A few more towns, in their bed of dark loam, and then it will be the Sahara. Bernis tonight will witness the laying to sleep of the earth.

Bernis feels dejected. Just two months earlier he was on his way to Paris to conquer Geneviève. Yesterday he reported back to duty, having put order in his defeat. These plains, these towns, these disappearing lights – it was he who was leaving them behind, who was casting them off. In an hour the beacon of Tangier would glow ahead of him; and until then for Jacques Bernis there was ample time to dream.

Part Two

I

I must go back and tell of those past two months, for otherwise what would be left of them? When the last faint ripples of the happenings I am going to describe will eventually have spent their force in ever-widening circles and, like the waters of a lake, have closed again over the lives they have blurred, when the emotions they aroused in me, at first so poignant, then less poignant, and finally almost tender, have been dulled, then all will once again seem right with the world. Cannot I already roam there where the memory of Geneviève and Bernis should be so cruel to me, without feeling more than a twinge of regret?

*

Two months earlier he was on his way to Paris; but after so long an absence it is not easy to feel at home again; one has the feeling of being one too many. He was simply Jacques Bernis dressed in a suit that smelled of moth-balls. He moved about in a body that felt sluggish and awkward, examining his packed belongings, too neatly parked in one corner of the room, to see what signs they gave of instability, impermanence. For this room was bare, as yet unsoftened by the charm of white sheets and books.

'Hallo ... It's you?' He began an inventory of his friendships. Exclamations of surprise, congratulations!

'So you're back! We'd almost given you up for good!'

'Yes, I'm back. When can I see you?'

Ah today, alas, we're busy. Well, tomorrow? Tomorrow – we'll be out on the golf links, but why not come out anyway? He doesn't care to? Well then, the day after. For dinner. Eight o'clock sharp.

He walked into a dance-hall without taking off his coat, a heavy-footed explorer among all these gigolos. Bottled up in this precinct they lead their little lives, like goldfish in an aquarium; they whisper sweet nothings, dance, and then come back to drink. In this vapid setting, where he alone kept his head, Bernis felt as heavy as a stevedore on his rigid legs. His thoughts were leaden. He threaded his way through the tables towards an empty seat. The female eyes he touched with his own shifted away and seemed to lose their lustre. The young men moved lithely back to let him pass. So at night, as the inspecting officer makes his rounds, do the cigarettes fall from the fingers of the sentinels on duty.

It was this world we used to find on each return, much as those Breton sailors return to find their postcard village and their too faithful sweetheart, hardly aged a day. Eternally the same, like an illustration in a children's picture book. On seeing everything so well in place, so well regulated by destiny, we were seized by some dim apprehension. Bernis asked about a friend. 'Oh yes, much the same as ever. Not doing too well in his business, though. Well, you know how it is . . . that's life!' All were captives of themselves, curbed by hidden reins and not, like himself, this fugitive, this poor child, this magician.

The faces of his friends were barely creased by two summers and two winters. He recognized the woman standing over there at one end of the bar, her face only faintly wearied from having served up so many smiles. The barman was the same as ever. He was afraid of being recognized by him, as though his voice, in calling out his name, might resuscitate a dead Bernis, a Bernis shorn of wings, a Bernis who never had escaped.

Slowly, during the flight back, an old familiar landscape had begun rising around him like a prison. The sands of the Sahara, the rocks of Spain had gradually retired, like scenic trappings. The frontier crossed at last and there was Perpignan, fed by its green plain, that plain on which the sun still lingered in oblique shafts of lengthening light, each passing minute more threadbare, more fragile, more transparent, as these golden vestments sank and evaporated into dust. Beneath the blue air he now looked down upon a soft, dark green ooze, a tranquil river bed. His engine idling, he sank towards this ocean bottom where all is still, where all is solid and as enduring as a wall.

And then the drive from the airfield to the station, with all those hard, closed faces opposite his own. All those hands on which fate had etched its lines and which now rested heavily on their owners' knees. And those peasants they had almost grazed, plodding homeward from the fields. And the young girl, waiting on her threshold for one man among a hundred thousand, who had forsworn a hundred thousand hopes. And that mother, cradling her infant in her arms, who was already its prisoner, who could never flee.

No manner of return could have been more intimate, no pathway have brought Bernis closer to the heart of things than this – his hands in his pockets, no suitcase to encumber him, an airman trekking home. Into the most immutable of worlds, where twenty years of legal wrangling were needed to lengthen a field or move a wall. After two years spent in Africa among shifting landscapes as ever-changing as the waves, here, having shed them one by one, he was back on his old home soil, the only one, the eternal one from which he was sprung. But it was a sorrowful archangel who thus set foot on solid ground.

'And here's everything just the same ...'

He had been afraid of finding things quite different, and now it pained him to find them so unchanged. The prospect of meeting people, of looking up old friends left him vaguely bored. From a distance fancy is free to roam. The tender friendships one gives up, on parting, leave their bite on the heart, but also a curious feeling of a treasure somewhere buried. What selfish love such flights occasionally attest! One night, in a Sahara peopled with stars, as he was dreaming of these tender friendships, so distant, so warm, and now so covered by the weather and the night, like seeds, he suddenly felt as though he had stepped aside to watch someone sleep. Propped against the stranded plane opposite that curve of sand, this dip in the skyline, he had found himself watching over his past loves like a shepherd.

'And I've come back to this!'

One day Bernis wrote to me: 'I won't speak of my homecoming. I feel myself in control of things when my emotions speak for me. But not one was aroused. I was like the pilgrim who reaches Jerusalem one minute too late. His yearning, his faith having died, all he finds are stones. This town here? A wall. I want to leave again. Do you recall our first departure? We made it together. Murcia, Granada, lying beneath us like showcase jewels and – since we didn't land – buried in the past. Deposited there, high and dry, by the ebbing tide of centuries. The engine was making that dense all-engulfing sound behind which the landscape streams by in silence, like a film. And the cold – for we were flying high up – and those towns caught in ice. Do you remember?

'I've kept the little slips of paper you kept passing up to me. "Watch out for that strange rattle . . . If it gets worse don't try to cross the Straits."

'Two hours later, as we neared Gibraltar, there was another. "Wait till you reach Tarifa before crossing – it's easier." At Tangier: "Come in for an early landing. Ground's soft."

'Nothing more. With sentences like that one can master the world. Your terse orders gave me a sense of forceful strategy at work. Tangier, that one-horse town, was my first conquest. My first theft. Vertical at first, and from so far. Then, during the descent, there was that blossoming of meadows, houses, flowers. I was hauling up a sunken city, sprung magically to life. And then suddenly that marvellous discovery: five hundred yards from the field an Arab bent over his plough whom I was pulling up towards me, making into a man of my own measure, who was really my booty, my fancy, my creation. I had taken a hostage and Africa was mine.

'Two minutes later, standing on the grass, I felt young, as though put down on some star where life begins anew. In that new climate, on that ground, under that sky I felt like a young tree. I stretched my flight-cramped muscles with a marvellous craving. I took long, flexible strides to unlimber from the piloting, and I laughed at having rejoined my shadow on landing.

'And that springtime! Do you remember that springtime after the drizzle of Toulouse? A new and vivifying air circulating among all things. Each woman contained a secret – a certain accent, a gesture, a form of silence. And all were equally desirable. And then – you know how I am – that haste to be off again and to search elsewhere for what I vaguely surmised but did not understand. For I was that diviner whose forked branch trembles and which he carries over the wide world until the treasure is found.

'But tell me what it is I seek and why here at my window, as I look out over this city – the city of my friends, my yearnings, my memories – I so despair? Why for the first time I find no wellspring and feel so far removed from the treasure? What was that obscure promise I was made and which some obscure god has failed to keep?'

*

'I've found the wellspring. Do you remember? It's Geneviève.'

*

When I read these words of Bernis's, I closed my eyes, Geneviève, and saw you once again as a little girl. Fifteen years old when we were thirteen. How in our reminiscences could you possibly have aged? You had remained that frail child, and it was she, when we heard speak of you, whom we had to imagine, to our surprise, launched upon the seas of life. While others escorted to the altar someone who was already a woman, it was a little girl whom Bernis and I, from the depths of Africa, imagined to be engaged. At fifteen you were the youngest of mothers. At an age when one scratches one's bare shins on branches, you were already demanding a real cradle, a queenly toy. And while for your elders, who could not guess the prodigy, you were making the humble, real-life gestures of a woman, for us you were living out a fairy tale and entering the world through a magic door – as in a masquerade, a children's ball – disguised as wife, mother, fairy.

For you were a fairy – how well I remember. Behind those thick old walls you lived in an aged house. I can see you again leaning out from the window, cut like an embrasure, and watching for the moon. As it rose, the plain began to rustle, the wings of the cicadas to rasp, the stomachs of the frogs to croak, and the returning oxen to ring their cow-bells. Still the moon rose. Sometimes the sound of a knell would come from the village, bringing to the crickets, the wheatfields, and the grasshoppers the news of an inexplicable death. And you leaned out, anxious only for the betrothed, for nothing is so threatened as hope. Still the moon rose. Whereupon the owls, outscreeching the knell, made love calls to one another, while below, the roving dogs gathered in a circle to bark at her. Still the moon rose. Then you would take our hands and you would tell us to listen, for those were the sounds of the earth, reassuring and good.

You were so well sheltered by that house and its living robe of earth. You had sealed so many pacts with the lindens and the oaks and the flocks that we called you their princess. Bit by bit your face grew soft as, towards evening, the world was put away for the night. 'The farmer has brought in his animals.' You knew it from the distant lights of the stables. A dull clang: 'They're closing the sluices.' Everything was in order. Finally the seven-o'clock express made its stormy passage through the gloaming, ridding our province and your world of all that is restless, mobile, uncertain – like a face peering from the window of a sleeping-car. Dinner followed in a dining-room that was too big and badly lit and where you became the Queen of the Night – for we were watching you like spies. Silently you would sit down among the grown-ups, in the midst of all that panelling, and leaning slightly forward so that your hair was caught in the golden hoop of the lampshades, you would reign over us, crowned in light. To us you seemed eternal, so closely were you linked to things, so sure were you of everything, your thoughts, your future. And thus you reigned.

But we wanted to know if it was possible to make you suffer, to press you tightly in our arms to the point of choking you; for we sensed in you a human presence we longed to bring to light. A tenderness, a distress we longed to bring out in your eyes. And Bernis would take you in his arms and you would blush. And Bernis would press you tighter and your eyes would grow bright with tears, without your lips being disfigured, as happens when old ladies weep. And Bernis would tell me that those tears came from the brimming heart, that they were more precious than diamonds, and that he who drank them would be immortal. He would also tell me that you inhabited your body like that underwater fairy, and that he knew a thousand spells to bring you to the surface, the surest being to make you cry. In this way we sought to steal you away from love. But the moment we let you go, you would laugh and this laughter would fill us with dismay. Thus a bird, when less tightly held, flies away.

'Geneviève, read us a poem.'

You read little, but we thought you already knew everything. We had never seen you startled.

'Read us a poem.'

You read, and what it taught us about the world and life came, we felt, not from the poet but from your wisdom. And the despairs of lovers and the tears of queens were transmuted, by the same magic, into the most tranquil things. One died of love with such calm in your voice.

'Geneviève, is it true one can die of love?'

You paused and pondered. Doubtless you sought the answer among the ferns, the crickets, and the bees, and you answered 'Yes', since the bees die of it. So it is ordained, so it must be.

'Geneviève, what is a lover?'

We wanted to make you blush. But you did not blush. Almost as light-footed as the moon, you gazed at its trembling reflection in the pond. For you, we thought, a lover was that light.

'Geneviève, do you have a lover?'

This time, surely, you would blush. But no. You smiled without embarrassment and shook your head. In your kingdom one season brings the flowers, autumn brings fruit, a season too brings love: life is simple.

'Geneviève, do you know what we'll do when grown up?' We wanted to dazzle you, and we called you – weak woman. 'Weak woman, we'll be conquerors!' We explained to you what life was – how the conquerors return laden with glory and make mistresses of those they love.

'So we shall be your lovers. Slave, read us a poem!'

But you had stopped reading and lain the book aside. You were suddenly so sure of your life, as a young tree might feel its growth and the seed bursting towards the light within it. This necessity was all that mattered. We were fairy-tale conquerors, but your roots were planted among your ferns, your bees, your goats, your stars, you harkened to the croak of your frogs, you drew your confident strength from all this lush life that was surging up around you in the hush of the night as in yourself, from toes to neck, towards that inscrutable yet certain fate.

Now that the moon was riding high and bedtime come, you closed the window and the moon shone in from behind the pane. We would say you had closed the sky like a shop-window, imprisoning the moon and a handful of stars; for we sought by all manner of traps and symbols to drag you down beneath appearances to those ocean depths towards which our restless beings called us.

*

'... I've found the wellspring, what I needed to recover from the journey. Here, close by. The others ... There are women, we used to say, who having been made love to, are rejected, banished to the outer stars, who were never more than a construction of the heart. Geneviève ... do you remember? ... was, we used to say, "inhabited". I have rediscovered her as one rediscovers the meaning of things, and I walk by her side in a world where at last I find myself at home ...'

She came to him as an envoy from the world of things. She was the go-between after a thousand ruptures, the match-maker for a thousand reconciliations. She gave him back those horse-chestnuts, that boulevard, that fountain. Once again each thing enclosed that secret which is its soul. The park was no longer combed, shaved, and brushed, as for an American; instead, the dried leaves marked the disorder of its lanes, and a fallen handkerchief bespoke the ambling footsteps of lovers. And thus did the park become a trap.

2

She had never spoken of Herlin, her husband, but this evening she said to Bernis: 'We've got a boring dinner party, Jacques, a mob of people. But if you'll join us, I'll feel less lonely.'

Herlin, as usual, was expansive, too much so. Why all this bombast which he would discard the moment they were alone? She watched him with misgiving. It was a made-up personality he flaunted – less from vanity than to give himself assurance.

'Your point, my dear fellow, is well taken.' Geneviève looked away. The pompous gesture, the tone of voice, the show of bluffness sickened her.

'Waiter! Some cigars!'

Never had she seen him so exuberant, so drunk, it seemed, with his power. In a restaurant, as on a podium, one is master of the world. A couple of words, and an idea is stood on its head. A couple of words, and the waiter and *maître d'hôtel* are sent bustling.

Geneviève half smiled to herself. Why this political dinner party? Why for the last six months this sudden passion for politics? Herlin had only to emit 'strong thoughts' to feel himself strong, in attitude no less than words. Then he could step back a pace and admire his own statue.

Leaving them to their game she turned to Bernis:

'Tell me, prodigal son, about the desert ... When will you be coming home for good?'

Bernis looked at her. Behind the unfamiliar mask of womanhood he glimpsed a fifteen-year-old girl smiling at him as in a fairy-tale. A child bent on hiding its secrets, but whose merest gesture betrays ... Geneviève, now I recall the spell: I shall have to take you in my arms and hug you till it hurts and then you'll cry and be yourself again...

The gentlemen now leaned towards Geneviève in a display of starched-shirt gallantry – as though a woman could be won through this competitive display of glittering metaphors and phrases. Her husband went out of his way to be charming. He rediscovered her now that others wanted her – thanks to that desire to please, that elegance, the dazzle of the evening dress which suggested the courtesan behind the woman. She thought: it's the mediocre which attracts him. Why would she never be loved entirely? Only one part of her was loved, the other left in shadow. She was loved as men love music, luxury. She had only to be witty or sentimental, and she made them want her. But what she believed in, what she felt, what she carried within her – they couldn't have cared a fig about. Her love for her child, her understandable anxieties – all this remained in shadow and was ignored.

Next to her each man became spineless, waxing indignant with her, feeling pity for her. Each seemed to say to her: 'I'll be the man you want.' And he meant it. For none of this was of any real importance. The only thing that would have mattered was ... going to bed with her.

Love was not constantly on her mind – she hadn't time for it. She recalled the first days of their engagement, and it made her smile. Herlin had suddenly discovered that he was in love (he had doubtless forgotten it?). He wanted to talk to her, to tame her, to win her. 'No, really, I haven't time! ...' She was walking down the path in front of him, nervously flicking at the branches with a stick in tempo with a song. The moist earth smelled good, the branches showered raindrops on their faces. She kept repeating: 'I haven't time ... no time!' First, she must hurry to the hothouse to look after her flowers.

'Geneviève, what a cruel girl you are!'

'Yes. I know. Look at my roses. See how heavily they hang! A lovely thing, a heavily hanging flower.'

'Geneviève, let me kiss you.'

'Of course. Why not? Do you like my roses?'

Men always loved her roses.

'No, really, my little Jacques, I'm not sad.' She leaned towards Bernis. 'I remember ... I was a funny little girl. I had invented a God of my own. Whenever I was overcome by some childish despair, I'd cry all day long. But once the light was blown out at night, I'd seek out my friend in prayer: "Look what has happened to me. I've spoiled my life and I'm much too weak to mend it. I give it all to you. You're much stronger than me. It's up to you to put things right." After which I went to sleep.'

Yes, amid so many untrustworthy things, so many still obeyed her. She reigned over books, flowers, friends, and sealed pacts with them. She knew the sesame for smiles, the sole password to the heart. 'Ah, it's you, my old astrologer ...' Or when Bernis came in: 'Sit down, you prodigal son ...' Each was bound to her by a secret, by the soft insight of complicity. The purest of friendships thus acquired the richness of a crime.

'Geneviève,' Bernis said to her, 'you still reign over everything.'

She had only to push back a table or draw up a chair and the delighted friend found himself perfectly at home. When the long day's work was done, what a silent tumult of scattered music, of damaged flowers – the ravages that friendship brings. Soundlessly, Geneviève restored peace to her kingdom. And Bernis could feel how distant in her and how well defended was the little captive girl who once had loved him ...

But one day her world was turned topsy-turvy.

3

'Do let me sleep!'

'What – sleep! Get up. The child is choking.'

Torn from her slumbers, she ran to the cot, where the child lay sleeping. His face was bright with fever, his breath short but calm. In her half-sleep Geneviève was reminded of a tugboat's panting puffs. 'What effort!' And for three days now it had been like this! Not knowing what to do, she stood bent over the child.

'Why did you say he was choking? Why did you frighten me so?'

Her heart was still beating wildly from the shock.

'I thought he was,' replied Herlin.

She knew he was lying. Seized by a sudden anxiety, incapable of suffering in solitude, he had made her share his anguish. That the world should rest in peace while he suffered was more than he could bear. Yet, after three sleepless nights, she needed rest. Already she hardly knew what she was doing.

She forgave him this recurrent blackmail because words, after all ... how little they mattered! And how ridiculous this strict accountance with sleep!

'You're being unreasonable,' she contented herself with saying, then added, more gently: 'You're a child.'

She turned abruptly to the nurse and asked the time.

'Two-twenty.'

'Ah ... two-twenty!' Geneviève repeated, as though there was something urgent to be done. But there was nothing. All one could do was wait, as on a trip. She smoothed the bed, rearranged the medicine bottles, touched the window, weaving about her an invisible, mysterious order.

'You should sleep a bit,' the nurse suggested.

Then silence. Again she was oppressed by this feeling of a journey, with the invisible landscape scudding past outside.

'This child we've watched growing, this child we've cherished ...' Herlin was now declaiming. He wanted Geneviève to pity him – in the rôle of grief-stricken father.

'Please, find something to do,' Geneviève gently counselled him. 'You've got a business appointment. So go!'

She gave his shoulders a soft push, but he was bent on nursing his grief.

'Why, the idea! At a moment like this ...'

At a moment like this, thought Geneviève, but ... but now more so than ever! She was overcome by an odd need for tidiness. That vase someone had moved, this overcoat of Herlin's draped over a chair, the dust over there on the shelf ... were so many marches stolen by the enemy. Obscure portents of doom. Of the doom against which she was battling. The dustless gilt of the *bric-à-brac*, the chairs in their proper places were bright facets of reality. Everything that was healthy, neat, and shining seemed to Geneviève to shield her against the darkness that is death.

'Things may improve. He's a sturdy little fellow,' the doctors kept saying. Of course. When sleeping he clung to life with two tiny clenched fists. It looked so pretty, so solid.

'Madame, you should go out a bit, stretch your legs,' the nurse repeated. 'I'll go out later. Otherwise, we'll both of us collapse.'

Strange, this sight of a child wearing out two women; a child who, with closed eyes and short breath, was dragging them to the ends of the earth.

Geneviève went out – to get away from Harlin's interminable lectures. 'My elementary duty . . . Your pride . . .' She understood nothing of these phrases, being half drugged with sleep; but certain words – like 'pride' – astonished her none the less. Why 'pride'? What had that to do with it?'

The doctor was puzzled by this young woman who shed no tears, did not utter an unnecessary word, and who waited on him with the precision of a nurse. He admired this devotion to life. And for Geneviève these visits were the happiest moments of the day. Not that he consoled her – he said nothing – but because, when he was present, the little child's body was precisely weighed and judged. Because everything serious, dark, unhealthy was clearly defined. What protection in this battle against the shadows!

It was even true of the operation of two days before. Groaning, Herlin had gone off to the drawing-room, but she had stayed on. The surgeon had come into the bedroom in his white smock with the powerful tranquillity of daylight. He and his assistant began a rapid battle. Curt words and orders: *chloroform* ... then *tighter* ... then *iodine* ... uttered in undertones, devoid of all emotion. And suddenly, like Bernis in his plane, she had an inkling of a forceful strategy: they would win through in the end.

'How can you watch all that?' Herlin had said to her. 'You must be a heartless mother!'

One morning, in the doctor's presence, she collapsed at the

foot of an armchair. When she came to, he did not offer her a word of courage or hope, nor did he show the slightest compassion. He looked at her gravely and said: 'You're overdoing it. It's ridiculous. I order you to go out this afternoon. Don't go to the theatre – people are so thick-witted they wouldn't understand – but do something like it.' And to himself he thought: 'This is the truest thing I've ever seen.'

*

Outside on the boulevard it was surprisingly cool. As she walked along she experienced a deep tranquillity in recalling her childhood. Trees and plains – simple things. One day, much later, this child had come to her and it was something at once incomprehensible and simpler still. The most cogent evidence of all. She had tended this child alongside of and among other living things. There were no words to describe what she had immediately felt. She had felt – but yes, just that – intelligent. Sure of herself, linked to everything, part of a universal concert. That evening she had had herself carried over to the window. The trees were alive and soaring, sucking up the springtime from the ground. She was their equal. Her child by her side was breathing ever so faintly, and this faint breath was the pulse and motor of the world.

But what havoc these last three days had wrought! The slightest gesture – like opening or closing a window – was now fraught with perplexities. She no longer knew what action to take. She fingered the bottles, the sheets, the child, uncertain of its import of such gestures in a world grown dark.

She passed an antique shop. Geneviève thought of the knick-knacks in her drawing-room as traps for the sunlight. Everything that retains the light, that rises brightly to the surface gave her pleasure. She paused to savour the silent smile in that piece of crystal glassware – the smile that gleams at one from a rare old wine. In her weary consciousness light, health, and the certainty of life were all intermingled; and she longed to brighten the room of her sinking child with this reflected sunbeam, pinned there like a golden nail.

4

Herlin returned to the attack. 'What! You're heartless enough to go out and amuse yourself, looking at antique shops! I'll never forgive you! It's . . .' he groped for the word – 'why, it's monstrous, unbelievable, unworthy of a mother!' Without thinking he had pulled a cigarette out of a red case, which he kept waving in the air. '. . . one's self-respect! . . .' Geneviève heard him repeat, wondering to herself: 'Is he going to light that cigarette?'

'Yes . . .' went on Herlin slowly, having kept this revelation for the end. 'Yes . . . and while the mother's out amusing herself, the child's vomiting blood.'

Geneviève turned deathly pale. She tried to leave the room, but he barred the door. 'Stay here!' He was panting, swiftly, like a beast. He was going to make her pay for this anguish he had had to endure alone!

'You're going to hurt me, and later you'll regret it,' said Geneviève simply.

But this remark, aimed at the fatuous windbag he was in the face of grave events, only spurred on his pent-up outburst. Yes, he ranted at her, she had always been indifferent to his efforts, light-headed, coquettish. Yes, for a long time he'd been fooled by her, he, Herlin, who had placed all his trust in her. Yes, and all for nothing! He had had to suffer for it all alone, for in life one is always alone!

Exasperated, Geneviève turned away, but he swung her sharply round, saying to her between his teeth: 'But there comes a time when women's failings catch up with them.' And as she still sought to slip from his grasp, he added this final enormity: 'The child is dying. God's finger is upon him.'

In a flash his anger fell, as though he had just struck a murderous blow. His own words left him gaping. White as a sheet, Geneviève made a move towards the door. He guessed the dreadful impression he had made on her, when his one desire had been to appear noble. Desperately he sought to undo this hideous image and to replace it by a gentler one.

'Excuse me ... Come back ... I must have been mad!' he stammered in a broken voice.

Half turned towards him, with her hand on the doorknob, she looked like a wild animal about to flee if he moved. He stood quite still.

'Listen ... I must talk to you ... it isn't easy ...'

She did not stir. What was she frightened of? The futility of her fright annoyed him. He wanted to tell her that he was out of his mind, cruel, unjust, that she alone was true and real, but first she must come closer and show her trust. Then he could humiliate himself before her. Then she would understand ...

But no, here she was, turning the knob. He shot out his arm and seized her brusquely by the wrist. She looked at him with crushing scorn. It made him angrier. He was determined to daunt her, to show her his strength, so that he could say: 'See – I've relaxed my grip.'

He pulled first gently, then more harshly on the fragile arm. She raised her hand to slap him, but he caught the other wrist in mid-air. Now he was hurting her, and he knew it. He was reminded of those children who seize a stray cat, wanting to tame it, and almost strangle it in their imperious desire to stroke it, to show it kindness. He heaved a sigh. 'I'm hurting her, I'm ruining everything.' For several seconds he felt a mad impulse to strangle Geneviève and with her the hideous impression he had made on her and of which he too was scared.

Finally he relaxed his fingers with a strange feeling of impotence and emptiness. She moved away from him slowly, as though he were no longer to be feared and she had suddenly been placed beyond his reach. He had ceased to exist. Pausing on the threshold, she quietly settled her hair and then, proudly erect, walked out.

That evening, when Bernis came to see her, she breathed not a word about it. Such things must be kept to oneself. Instead, she had him talk of his recollections of their common childhood, and of his life out there. It was a little girl she was entrusting to his care, a little girl to be consoled with pictures.

She leaned her forehead on his shoulder and Bernis thought that all of Geneviève was thus running to him for shelter. Doubtless she thought it too. Doubtless they both thought it, not realizing that in a casual caress one commits but a small part of oneself.

5

'Geneviève, what's the matter? . . . You here at such an hour? . . . But heavens! How pale you are!'

Geneviève said nothing, listening to the infuriating tic-tac of the clock. Already the lamp's pale light was fading into the sickly, ashen brew of dawn. The sight of the window sickened her.

'I saw a light . . . and I came up . . .' she said with an effort, but could find nothing more to add.

'Yes, Geneviève, I . . . I was reading, as you can see . . .'

The paper-bound volumes stood out in splashes of yellow, white, and red – like strewn petals, thought Geneviève. Bernis waited, but she did not move.

'I was day-dreaming in that armchair, Geneviève. I opened one book, then another, but I had the impression of having read them all.'

He sounded this world-weary note to conceal his excitement, adding in as calm a voice as he could: 'What's on your mind, Geneviève?'

When in his heart he thought – this is a miracle of love.

Geneviève wrestled with a single, overpowering thought: 'He doesn't know.' Looking at him in astonishment she added out loud: 'I've come ...' and passed her hand across her forehead.

The window panes grew whiter, flooding the room with a bleak, aquarium light. 'The lamp is fading,' thought Geneviève, then suddenly burst out: 'Jacques, Jacques, take me away!'

Bernis turned pale. He took her in his arms and began rocking her like a child. She closed her eyes.

'You'll take me away ...'

On his shoulder she could feel time flowing by without hurting her. It was almost a joy to renounce everything, abandon oneself to the current; it was as though her own life were ebbing out and away – 'without hurting me', she dreamed out loud.

Bernis stroked her face. A thought crossed her mind. 'Five years ... five years ... yet it happened! And I gave him so much ...'

'Jacques! ...Jacques ... My son is dead.'

*

'I've left the house, you see. I need peace so badly – oh, so badly! I still haven't grasped it, I don't yet feel the pain. Am I a heartless woman? The others cry and would like to console me. They're moved to tears by their own kindness. But I ... I haven't had time to remember ...

'To you I can say everything. Death comes in a terrible muddle – injections, bandages, telegrams. After several sleepless nights one walks around in a daze. During the doctor's visits all I could do was lean my empty head against the wall ...

'And all those arguments with my husband, what a nightmare! Today, or rather yesterday ... he caught me by the wrist and I thought he was going to twist it. All because of an injection –when I knew the time for it hadn't yet come. Then he begged my forgiveness. As though it mattered! "Yes", I answered, "yes ... Let me go back to my son." But he blocked the door, saying: "Forgive me. I need your forgiveness." There was no getting it out of his head. "Look, let me go," I said. "I forgive you." To which he replied: "Yes, with your lips, but not with your heart." And on it went – enough to drive me mad.

'So when it's all over, one doesn't feel a great despair. Just a peace, a silence which almost comes as a surprise. I kept thinking, thinking: the child is resting. Nothing more. I also had the impression of getting off a boat at dawn, far off, I don't know where, and I no longer knew what to do. I kept thinking: "We've arrived." I looked at the syringes and medicine bottles and thought to myself: "It no longer makes sense. We've arrived." And then I fainted ...'

Suddenly she started up: 'It was mad of me to come.'

Back there, she sensed, the dawn was rising greyly on a great disaster. The sheets were cold, the beds unmade; there were towels lying on the chest of drawers, a chair lay on its side, upset. She must hurry back to oppose this on-surging débâcle. There was that armchair, that vase, that book to be pushed back into place. Vain it might be, but she must needs restore order to life's props.

6

There were the usual calls and expressions of condolence. It is difficult to speak without striking a pose; and the sad memories which were thus stirred up within her were left to settle in an awkward silence. She carried her head high, and without faltering she uttered the word everyone was carefully side-stepping – death. She wasn't going to let them catch in her own speech echoes of their own tentative phrases. She looked them straight in the eyes, so that they would not dare look at her, but as soon as she lowered her own . . .

Then there were the others – those who walked with a calm, tranquil step across the hall, but who, on entering the drawing-room, took several hurried steps and fell into her arms. She offered them not a word. They choked her grief, pressing to their bosoms a contorted child.

Already her husband was talking of selling the house. 'These sad memories hurt us,' he explained. He lied, for suffering is almost a friend. But it enabled him to stir up a fuss, strike dramatic poses. This evening he was to leave for Brussels, where she was to join him. 'If you only knew the mess the house is in . . .'

All her past was now upset. Beginning with the drawing-room, which a long patience had composed. With the furniture decanted there, not by merchants but by time. But move that armchair away from the fireplace, separate that console table from its wall, and everything is stripped of its past, appearing naked for the first time.

'And you, I suppose, will be leaving too?' she said, with a gesture of despair.

A thousand pacts now broken! Was it then a child who had bound everything together, around whom her world revolved? A child whose death was such a defeat for Geneviève? She broke down: 'I'm so miserable . . .'

Bernis spoke softly to her. 'I'll take you away. I'll carry you off. Do you remember? . . . I used to say that one day I'd return. I used to say . . .'

Bernis pressed her in his arms, and Geneviève, her head thrown back a bit, had her eyes brim-full of tears. It was a little sobbing girl whom Bernis now held captive in his arms.

*

Cape Juby, (dated)

Bernis, old boy, today is mail day. The plane has left Cisneros. Soon it will touch down here and take away to you these mild words of reproach. I've thought a lot about your letters and our captive princess. Yesterday, while walking on the empty beach, so nude, so empty, so eternally sea-washed, it occurred to me that we too are like that. I wonder if really we exist. There have been evenings when, in the half light of tragic sunsets, you have seen the Spanish fort sink in the lustre of the shining sands. But the mysterious blue of their reflections is not of the same stuff as the fort. Yet that is your realm. Not very real, anything but sure... But let Geneviève live.

Yes, in her present distress, I know... But tragedies in real life are rare. There are so few real friendships, affections, loves to be lost. Say what you will about Herlin, a man counts but little. Life, I think... is based on something else.

These customs, these conventions, these laws – everything you don't feel the need of, everything you ran away from – all this is what gives her life a framework. To exist, one must have about one realities which last. But absurd or unjust, all this is but mere words. And Geneviève, carried off by you, will no longer be Geneviève.

Besides, does she really know what it is she needs? That habit of fortune, of which she's unaware. Money is what permits the conquest of goods, external agitation – and her life is internal – but fortune is that which makes things last. It is the invisible, subterranean stream, which for a century nourishes the walls of a mansion, one's memories, the soul. And you are going to empty her life as one empties an apartment of the thousand objects one no longer noticed but of which it was composed.

But for you, I fancy, to love is to be born. You will imagine yourself carrying off a new Geneviève. Love, for you, is that particular shade in the eyes which you occasionally glimpsed in her and which can be nourished easily enough, as one nourishes a lamp. And it is true that at certain moments the simplest words seem charged with such power that it is easy to nourish love.

But living, undoubtedly, is something else again...

7

Geneviève felt embarrassed to run her fingers over this curtain and that armchair, like new-found landmarks. Up till now her fingerings had been a game. This décor up till now had seemed so light that its movements had resembled the coming or going of stage scenery. She whose taste was so sure had never wondered what this Persian carpet was, nor this *toile de Jouy* wallpaper. Up until today they formed the soft image of an interior, and only now for the first time did she see them.

'It's only natural,' she thought. 'I'm still only a stranger in a life which isn't mine.' She sank back into an armchair and closed her eyes, as though seated in the compartment of an express train. With each passing second houses, villages, and forests are being whirled back behind; yet each time one opens one's eyes in the sleeper, the same brass hook is there before one. One is transformed, but without knowing it. 'In a week's time I'll open my eyes and – since he's carrying me away – I'll be a new person.'

'What do you think of our abode?'

Why waken her so soon? She looked about, not knowing how to express her feelings: this décor seemed transient, and its frame to lack solidarity.

'Come closer, Jacques, you who are real...'

This half-light playing on the sofas, these bachelor apartment hangings, the Moroccan fabrics strung up on the walls – there was nothing here that could not be put up or removed in just five minutes.

'Jacques, why do you hide your walls like this? Why do you want to soften the contact between walls and fingertips?'

There was nothing she loved more than running her palm over the raw stone, caressing that which in a house is most solid and enduring. That which can hold you up for a long time, like a ship...

He showed her his treasures, his 'souvenirs'. She understood. She had known Colonial Army officers who, coming back to Paris, lived the lives of phantoms. They bumped into each other on the boulevards and were amazed to see each other still alive. Their dwelling places were made up of this house in Saigon, of that villa in Marrakesh. They talked of women, old officer friends, new promotions; but the draperies which overseas might have been the living tissue of the walls here seemed dead.

She fingered some slender brasswork.

'Don't you like my mementos?'

'Excuse me, Jacques ... they're a bit ...' She dared not say 'vulgar'. But that sureness of taste which came from her having known and loved genuine Cézannes, as opposed to copies, real antique furniture rather than imitations, made it hard for her not to look down on these humble objects. She was ready to sacrifice everything in the most generous of impulses; she could, she thought, have endured life in a white-washed cell, but here she felt she was compromising something within her. Not the delicacy of the rich-born child that she was, but – how strange – her very integrity. He sensed her embarrassment without understanding it.

'Geneviève, I can't offer you as many comforts, I'm not...'

'But Jacques, you're mad! What did you think? I couldn't care less ...' She nestled in his arms. 'Only, I'd rather have a simple well-waxed floor in the place of your rugs ... But I'll arrange it for you.'

She broke off suddenly, realizing that the nakedness she craved was a far greater luxury, requiring much more of objects than the masks with which they were covered here. The hallway where she had played as a child, those gleaming walnut floors, those massive tables which had traversed centuries without ageing or growing outmoded...

She was overcome by a strange feeling of melancholy. Not that she regretted her past fortune and all it had made possible. Probably the superfluous had played a smaller rôle in her life than in Jacques', but she understood that in her new life she would be rich above all in superfluities. When she didn't need them. But what she would not have was this assurance of longevity. Those objects, she thought, lasted longer than I. They welcomed me, escorted me through life, and would one day keep vigil over my remains. But now I am going to outlive the things around me.

'When I used to go to the country ...' she thought, conjuring up in her mind's eye the façade of that house beyond the thick lindens. Its most stable feature was there for all to see: those terraced steps whose massive stones were rooted in the earth. There, she thought, the winter ... the winter cleans the forest of dry wood and lays bare the house's silhouette: the framework of a house, the very framework of the world.

On her way out she would whistle to her dogs. The dead leaves crackled underfoot; but winter having undertaken this extensive pruning, she knew that spring would replenish the empty warp, climb the branches, burst open the buds, and renew those green vaults which have the depth and movement of deep waters.

There something of her son still lingered on. Stepping into the barn, to turn the half-ripe quinces, she would catch him sneaking away; now, after all this running around, my little one, after all this mad scampering, wouldn't it be wiser to go to bed?

There she knew the language of the dead and was not afraid of it. Each added his silence to the silence of the house. One raised one's eyes from one's book, one held one's breath, one hearkened to the call that had just expired. Why call them the departed when, among those that change, they alone are durable and their last looks so true that nothing else they did could ever gainsay them?

'Now I shall follow this man, I shall suffer and have doubts about him.' For she had only been able to sort out this human confusion of tenderness and harsh rebuffs in those who had found their quietus.

She opened her eyes and saw that Bernis was dreaming.

'Jacques, you must protect me. I'm going away so poor, so poor!'

She would survive that house in Dakar, the Buenos Aires crowd, in a world where nothing had the character of necessity and where, if Bernis' strength should fail him, nothing would seem more real than pictures in a book.

He bent over and spoke to her tenderly. Yes, she must try to believe in this image he was offering of himself, of this divinely-inspired tenderness. She was ready to love love's image; she had only this weak image to defend her. Tonight, in a moment of fleeting rapture, she would seek out this weak shoulder and bury her face in this weak refuge, like some wild wounded creature preparing to die.

8

'Where are you taking me? Why have you brought me here?'

'You don't like this hotel, Geneviève? Shall we try somewhere else?'

'Yes, please ...' she said in a fearful voice.

The headlights were working badly. Painfully they bored on through the night, as through a hole. From time to time Bernis turned to glance at her. Geneviève seemed very pale.

'Are you cold?'

'A little, but it's nothing. I forgot to bring my fur.'

It began to rain. 'A stinker of an evening!' said Bernis to himself, still thinking that such are the approaches to the earthly paradise.

Near Sens they had to stop to change a sparkplug. He had forgotten the torch – one more thing forgotten. Under the dripping rain he fumbled with a slipping spanner. 'We should have taken the train,' he kept obstinately thinking. He had preferred his car because of the impression of freedom it gave. Lovely freedom! From the outset of this mad flight he'd committed nothing but stupidities. And all those things he'd left behind.

'Can you manage?'

Geneviève had joined him. Suddenly she felt a prisoner here: one tree, two trees watching over them like sentries, and that stupid little road-worker's shack. What a strange thought – were they going to spend their lives here?

The job done, he took her hand.

'Why, you're feverish!'

She smiled. 'Yes ... I'm a bit tired. I'd so like to sleep.'

'But why did you come out in the rain?'

The engine worked badly, spluttering and coughing.

'Jacques, darling, will we ever get there?' She was half asleep, wrapped in her fever. 'Will we ever get there?'

'But of course, my love, Sens is just ahead.'

She sighed. This effort was too much for her – and all because of a spluttering motor. Each tree was like a dead weight she had to pull towards her. One after the other, in endless repetition.

'Can't be,' thought Bernis, 'but we're going to have to stop again.' The prospect of a new breakdown appalled him. An immobilized landscape was more than he could take. He was nagged by dark thoughts: the powers of darkness were out to get him.

'Geneviève, my little one, don't think about tonight ... Think of the future ... Think of ... Spain. Do you think you'll like Spain?'

A weak voice answered him, speaking from afar: 'Yes, Jacques, I'm happy ... only ... I'm a bit scared of bandits.' He could see her smiling faintly. Bernis was upset by this little nothing of a phrase, which could only mean that their trip to Spain was a fairy-tale. She did not believe in it. What is an army without faith? An army without faith cannot win.

'Geneviève, it's this night, this rain that's undermining our confidence ...'

Suddenly this night seemed to him like an interminable illness. There was a sick taste in his mouth. It was one of those nights which hold out no hope of dawn. He fought the feeling, repeating to himself: 'Dawn would be a blessing if only it stops raining ... If only ...' There was something in them that had fallen ill, but he didn't know it. He thought it was the earth which had turned rotten, the night that was sick. He longed for the dawn, like those prisoners who say: 'When day comes I'll breathe again', or 'When spring returns I'll be young once more ...'

'Geneviève, think of the little house we'll have down there.'

Immediately he realized this was something he should not have said. There was no way of giving it reality in Geneviève's mind.

'Yes, our house ...' She tried out the word for sound. But she could put no heat into it, its savour was fleeting. Strange, unfamiliar thoughts floated through her head groping for the words to fit them, a swarm of thoughts that frightened her.

Knowing nothing of the hotels in Sens, he drew up under a lamp-post to consult his guidebook. A faint, flickering gaslight moved the shadows on the wall, showing up a ghostly shopsign, part of whose rain-washed words had disappeared: BIKES ... It struck him as the saddest and most vulgar word he'd ever seen. Symbol of a mediocre existence. Many things in his life out there must have been mediocre, only he hadn't noticed it.

'Eh, Bourgeois, got a light? ...'

Three scrawny kids were looking on and giggling. 'These Americans ... trying to find their road ...' Then they looked at Geneviève.

'Shove off, damn you!' growled Bernis.

'Nice bit of fluff you got there ... But you oughta see the one we've got at Number 29! ...'

Geneviève leaned nervously towards him. 'What are they saying? Please, please, let's drive on.'

'But Geneviève . . .' He made an effort and stopped short. After all, he had to find her a hotel. What did these tipsy youngsters matter? Then he remembered that she was feverish and in pain, that he should have spared her this encounter. He reproached himself with having exposed her to such ugly things. He . . .

The Hôtel du Globe was shut. At night all these little hotels looked like drapers' shops. He kept pounding on the door until at last some dragging footsteps approached from the other side. The night porter opened the door, a wee crack.

'Full up.'

'Please, my wife's ill,' Bernis pleaded. But the door had already closed. The footsteps disappeared up the hallway.

So everything was conspiring against them? . . .

'What did he say?' asked Geneviève. 'Why didn't he answer?'

Bernis felt like replying that this wasn't the Place Vendôme and that once these little hotels reached their fill, they went to sleep. What could be more normal? He climbed back in behind the steeringwheel without a word. His face was bathed in sweat. Instead of starting the engine, he stared at the glistening cobblestones as the rainwater trickled down his neck. He felt crushed by this leaden weight, by this lifeless world he must somehow rouse. And once again the silly idea came back – when dawn comes . . .

At this point a human word was needed, and it was Geneviève who tried it.

'It doesn't matter, darling. One must work for one's happiness.'

Bernis looked at her. 'Yes, you're so understanding.' He was deeply moved. He would have liked to kiss her, but this rain, this discomfort, this fatigue . . . He took her hand and found it even more feverish. Each second was undermining this frail body. He sought to calm himself by thinking: 'I'll make her a hot grog.

No, a piping hot grog. I'll wrap her up in blankets. We'll look at each other and laugh over the hardships of this trip.' He felt vaguely reassured. But how ill the immediate reality fitted this happy prospect! Two other hotels remained obstinately shut. Each rebuff made it harder for him to revive his desperate, his increasingly unreal imaginings.

Geneviève had lapsed into silence. He sensed that she would not complain nor utter another word. He could drive on for hours, for days, she would say nothing. Nothing more. He could twist her arm, she would still say nothing ... 'What's come over me? I must be dreaming!'

'Geneviève, my little one, are you feeling rotten?'

'But no, it's over. I feel better.'

She had just given up despairing of so many things. For whom? For him. Things he could never give her. This 'something better' was now a broken spring. She was more resigned now that she had given up hoping for happiness. In this way things could only get better. Until one day everything would be fine ... 'Fine! What a fool I am – dreaming again.'

They drew up in front of the Hôtel de l'Espérance et de l'Angleterre. Special rates for travelling salesmen.

'Lean on my arm, Geneviève ... Yes, we want a room. Madame is ill. And quick, bring us a hot grog! A piping hot grog.'

Special rates for travelling salesmen. Why did that phrase sound so dismal?

'Sit down in this armchair, darling, you'll feel better.'

Why was that grog so long arriving? Special rates for travelling salesmen.

The aged chambermaid bustled about her. 'There, my little dy. There, my poor Madame. She's all a-tremble, and so pale. I'll fetch a hot bottle. Number 14, it is, lovely big room ... And would Monsieur please fill out the forms?'

Holding the ink-stained pen in his fingers, he noticed that

their names were different. He didn't like the idea of exposing Geneviève to the condescending smiles of hotel porters. 'My fault – how tactless!'

She came to the rescue, once again. 'Lovers,' she said. 'Isn't that a tender word?'

They thought of Paris, of the scandal it would occasion, of all those severely shaking heads. A new and difficult experience was beginning for both of them, but they were careful not to speak, for fear of giving voice to the same apprehensions. And suddenly Bernis realized the insignificance of all they had so far had to face: nothing, nothing but a sluggish engine, a few raindrops, ten minutes lost looking for a hotel. The exhausting hardships they had had to overcome came only from themselves. It was against herself that Geneviève was struggling, and what was being torn from her was so deep-rooted that already she was maimed.

He took her hands, but realized once again the futility of words.

*

Now she slept. He was not thinking of love, but strange visions flickered across his mind. Reminiscences. The flame of the oil-lamp. Quick, it must be replenished. But the flame must also be shielded from the wind, from the high wind that's blowing ...

But above all, this detachment! He would have wished her more avid for the good things of this life. Racked by the lack of certain things and crying to be fed them, like a child. Then, for all his poverty, he would have had so much to give her. But how poor he now felt, kneeling before a child who was not hungry!

9

'No. Nothing... Let me be... Ah, already?'

Bernis had got up. In her dream his gestures had been as heavy as a wharfman's. Like the gestures of an apostle who drags you up from your own depths. Each of his steps was charged with meaning, like a dancer's. 'Oh, my love!'

He paced up and down, looking ridiculous. Dawn was now dirtying that window. The night had been dark blue. Beyond the lamp-light it had had the dark depth of a sapphire. A night dug so deep that it reached to the stars. Dreams. A Milky Way of fancies. One feels like a watchman, at the prow of a ship.

She drew her knees up against her body, her skin feeling pasty, like badly baked bread. Her heart was beating too quickly and it hurt her. Like the sound of wheels in a railway-carriage, pounding out the rhythm of one's flight. One presses one's forehead against the window and the landscape floats past – dark masses which the horizon quietly gathers in, envelops in its peace, gentle as death.

She would have liked to cry out to him: 'Hold me back!' The arms of love encompass you with your present, your past, your future, the arms of love gather you together.

'No. Let me be.'

She got up.

10

This decision, thought Bernis, has been taken by something other than ourselves. It had been taken without a word exchanged between them. As though the return had been agreed upon in advance. Dogged by sickness, they could not think of continuing. Later on . . . they'd see. For so brief an absence and with Herlin away, everything could be smoothed over. Bernis was surprised to discover how simple it all seemed. Yet he knew it wasn't so. It was the easiest way out, relieving them of further effort.

Besides, he mistrusted himself. He had yielded up to fancies once again. But from what depths do such fancies rise? This morning, waking up to find himself staring at that low, dark ceiling, he had thought: 'Her house was a ship, carrying generations from one side to the other. The crossing makes no sense, neither here nor anywhere else, but what security there is in having one's ticket, one's cabin, and one's bright leather suitcases. To feel one has set sail . . .'

He didn't yet know if he was distressed because he was embarked on a downward slope and could feel the future coming up to meet him without his having to exert himself. One's suffering disappears when one lets oneself go, when one yields – even to sadness. Later he would feel it more strongly, in picturing certain scenes. But for the moment they were playing out this second act in their rôles, because in some part of them it had all been foreseen. So he thought as he spurred on an engine that was as sluggish as ever. But they would get there. For they were now running downhill. Down the slope which coloured all his thinking.

Near Fontainebleau she felt thirsty. The details of the countryside were now familiar, reassuring – like a frame into which, quite naturally, one fitted.

In the roadside café where they stopped, they were given some warm milk. Why hurry? She drank it in short sips. Why hurry? Everything that was befalling them had been foreordained; it responded to that same image of necessity.

She was all gentleness, grateful to him for so much. Their relations were far less tense than they had been the day before. She smiled, pointing to a little bird that was pecking on the ground in front of the door. Her face seemed changed. Where had he seen this face before? ... Ah, yes, on the faces of travellers, travellers on station platforms who a moment later will have been wrenched from sight. Such faces can already smile, glowing with unexpected fervours.

He glanced at her once again. Her head, in profile, was bent. She was sunk in thought. If she turned her head, ever so little, she would be lost to him forever. She still loved him, no doubt, but one should not ask too much of a frail little girl. Obviously he couldn't say: 'I'm giving you back your freedom,' nor any other stupid phrase. Instead, he spoke of his plans, his future. In the life he thus conjured up she was not a captive.

To thank him, she placed her little hand on his arm. 'You're everything to me ... my love.'

It was true, but the words made him understand that they were not made for one another.

So gentle, yet so stubborn. So near to being hard, cruel, unjust, but without realizing it. So ready, so desperately ready to defend some obscure possession, while remaining calm and gentle.

Nor was she made for Herlin either. He knew it. The life she was talking of returning to had never brought her anything but pain. For what then was she made? She gave no sign of suffering.

They climbed back into the car. Bernis kept well over to his side. He too could stifle his suffering; but within him there was a wounded creature whose tears he could not comprehend.

Paris they found much the same, and their return changed nothing.

II

And all of this for what? Round about him the city kept up the same pointless hustle and bustle. Amid all this confusion he felt lost. Slowly he pushed upstream against this alien crowd, thinking to himself: 'It's as though I weren't here.' Soon he would be leaving; and a good thing too! His job, he knew, would tie him down with such material claims that his life would recover its sense of reality. He also knew that in day-to-day existence the slightest step assumes the importance of a fact, blunting the impact of a sentimental disaster. Even the rough mess-room jokes would have lost nothing of their flavour. It was curious, yet certain: he was no longer interested in himself.

As he was passing by Notre-Dame, he walked in, and was surprised to find such a crowd inside. He took refuge against a pillar. What was he doing here? – he wondered. After all, he had walked inside because here the passing minutes led to something. Outside they no longer led anywhere. That was it: 'Outside the minutes no longer lead anywhere.' He also felt the need to take stock of himself, and he offered himself up to faith as to any mental discipline. 'If only,' he said to himself, 'I can find a formula which sums me up, which makes me one, then for me it will be the truth.' To which he added wearily: 'But even so I wouldn't believe it.'

Suddenly it occurred to him that he was still on a cruise and that his entire life had been consumed in an attempted flight. The first words of the sermon disturbed him, like a ship's horn blowing the signal for departure.

'The Kingdom of Heaven,' began the preacher, 'the Kingdom of Heaven ...'

Resting his hands on the broad pulpit rim, he leaned forward over the crowd. A packed crowd ready to absorb everything, ready to be nourished. How apt the Biblical images which now swept over him! He thought of the fish caught in a net, and went on without transition: 'When the fisherman of Galilee ...'

The words he now used were all made to evoke a long and enduring train of reminiscences. Like a runner beginning to hit his stride, he exerted a slow but steady pressure on the crowd.

'Could you but know ... Could you but know the boundless love ...'

He paused, a bit out of breath. His feelings were too full to be expressed. Even the simplest, most threadbare words were charged with too much meaning for him to be able to distinguish those which really carry. In the light of the candles his face seemed made of wax. He drew himself up, his forehead raised, his hands still resting on the pulpit. When he relaxed, there was a stirring in the congregation, like a tremor in the sea.

Then the words came to him in a flood. He spoke with an astonishing assurance, with the light-heartedness of a stevedore enjoying his young strength. The ideas seemed to descend on him from above, like bales being passed to him even as he was finishing the previous sentence, and already he could vaguely feel welling up within him the image needed to be coined, the formula destined to convey the new idea to this public.

Bernis now listened to the peroration.

'I am the source, the fountainhead of life. I am the tide which enters into you, gives you life, and ebbs. I am the evil which enters into you, rends your hearts, and withdraws. I am the love which enters into you and which lasts for evermore.

'And you would brandish Marcion against me, along with the Fourth Gospel. And you come to me, speaking of interpolations. And you marshal against me your wretched human logic – when I am he who is beyond it, when I am come to deliver you from it!

'Oh prisoners, hearken unto me! I deliver you from your science, your formulas, your laws, from that bondage of the spirit, from that determinism which is more obdurate than fate. I am the cleft in the armour-plating. I am the loophole in the prison. I am the error in the calculation. I am life.

'You have integrated the movement of the stars, oh generation of the laboratories, but the stars themselves ye know not. They are become symbols in your books, yet they yield no light, and you know less about them than a little child. You have even laid bare the laws which govern human love, but this love itself eludes your prescriptions, and you know less about it than a young girl! Therefore come ye unto me, and I shall give you back this tenderness of light, this light of love. I do not enslave you; I save you. From the man who first calculated the fall of a fruit and locked you into this bondage I free you. My mansion is your sole refuge, and outside it what would you become?

'What would you become outside my mansion, outside this vessel wherein the passage of the hours is imbued with meaning, like the gush of the sea beneath the bowsprit. The silent ocean flux which draws the blessed islands closer. That ocean flux ...

'Come to me, all ye who have tasted the bitter fruit of vain endeavours. Come to me, you who have found bitter the thoughts which lead to iron laws ...'

He flung out his arms.

'For I am the Welcomer and Receiver. I have borne the sins of the world. I have borne its sufferings. I have borne the burden of your incurable maladies, I have borne your sorrows, akin to those of animals who lose their young, and your grief therein was lightened. But what ails you now, my people, is a deeper and more irreparable ill. Yet this too shall I bear, as I have the others. I shall bear the heavier chains of the spirit.

'For I am he who bears the burdens of the world.'

The man struck Bernis as desperate – because he did not cry out for a Sign, because he did not proclaim a Sign from on high. Because he was seeking to answer his own questions.

'And ye shall be as little children playing. So come unto me, ye who wear yourselves out in vain endeavours. I shall give them a meaning, they shall build in your hearts, and I shall make of them a human thing.'

The words penetrated the crowd. Bernis no longer heard

them, but only something which echoed in them like a leitmotif. 'And I shall make of them a human thing.'

He felt uneasy.

'Lovers of today, come unto me, and I shall make of your dried-up, cruel, and desperate loves a human thing.

'Come unto me, those of you who have known the lure of the flesh and been downcast, and I shall make a human thing ...'

Bernis felt even more uneasy.

'... For I am he who has looked upon man and marvelled ...'

Bernis felt shattered.

'I alone can give man back to himself.'

The priest stopped. Exhausted, he turned towards the altar, to worship the God he had just exalted. He felt humble, as though he had given everything, as though this exhaustion of his body were a gift. Unwittingly he had identified himself with Christ. Facing the altar, he went on, with agonizing slowness:

'Father, I had faith in them, therefore did I give up my life ...' And turning a last time towards the congregation, he added: 'For I love them ...'

He trembled. The silence filled Bernis with awe.

'In the name of the Father ...'

'What despair!' thought Bernis. 'But where is the act of faith? What I heard was no act of faith, only an utterly desperate cry.'

He walked out. Soon the arc-lamps would be lit. Bernis ambled along the banks of the Seine. The trees did not stir, their tangled branches caught in the amber dusk. Bernis walked on. A feeling of calm came over him, bestowed on him by this twilight truce, the peace which comes from a problem one thinks solved.

And yet this twilight was too theatrical. It had served as a backdrop for crumbling Empires, nights of defeat, and the climaxes of feeble loves; tomorrow it would serve for other comedies as well. Such a backdrop is disturbing if the evening is calm and life drags its feet – for then one no longer knows just what drama is brewing. Oh for something to save him from this so human anxiety!

The arc-lamps, all of them together, burst into light.

12

Taxis, buses. A nameless confusion where, Bernis, it is good to lose oneself? A dunderhead, blocking the pavement. 'Eh there, come on!' Women met just once in a lifetime: one's only chance. Up there Montmartre, with its harsher lights. Streetwalkers already on the job. 'For God's sake – be off!' Across the way women of a different sort. Hispano Suizas, like jewel-cases, able to give even to unlovely women the appearance of precious flesh. Five hundred thousand francs' worth of pearls dripping down to their navels, and what rings! A beautifully pampered flesh. But here's another streetwalker, with a fistful of complaints: 'Lemme go, I know you, you pimp, now scram! Quit pestering me, I gotta living to make!'

*

He stepped into a cabaret. At the next table a woman was having supper, in an evening dress cut into a V over her bare back. All he could see of her was that neck and those shoulders and the blind back which occasionally twitched with fleshy shivers. That ever recomposed, unseizable matter. Her head bent and her chin propped on her hand, she was smoking a cigarette, but all he could see of her was this bare expanse. Like a wall, he thought.

The dancing girls began their act. Their steps were lithe and the music of the ballet gave them a soul. Bernis enjoyed the rhythm which kept them poised in such exquisite balance. An ever threatened equilibrium which they regained each time with a startling assurance. They provoked the senses by forever undoing the image that was about to form, reducing it again to movements just as it hovered on the verge of immobility, of death. It was the very expression of desire.

In front of him the mysterious back was still there, smooth as the surface of a lake. But the slightest gesture, thought, or shiver sent waves of shadow rippling across it. 'What I need,' Bernis thought, 'is what moves darkly, below that surface.'

The dancing girls made their bows, having traced and then effaced a few enigmas in the sand. Bernis beckoned to the most light-footed among them.

'You dance well.' He could feel the weight of her body, like the flesh of a ripe fruit, and it was for him a revelation to find that she had substance. She sat down. Her gaze was steady and there was something ox-like in the set of her smooth neck, the least flexible of all her joints. Her face lacked finesse, but her body flowed away from it and was imbued with a sense of great repose.

Then Bernis noticed that her hair was moist with sweat. There was a wrinkle in her make-up, her apparel had lost its bloom. Withdrawn from the dance, as from an element, she seemed awkward and undone.

'A penny for your thoughts.' She made a diffident gesture.

All this nocturnal agitation now made sense. The bustling about of page-boys, cab-drivers, of the *maître d'hôtel* – they were all doing their job, which, when all was said and done, was simply to push towards him this tired girl and this bottle of champagne. Bernis was watching life from the wings of the stage, where all is business: where there is neither vice nor virtue, nor troubled emotion, but a toil as routine and dull as that of any team of men. Even that dance, which had woven disparate gestures into a language of its own, could only speak to a stranger. The stranger alone perceived in it an elaborate construction, which she and the others had long since forgotten. Thus the musician who plays the same air for the thousandth time forgets its meaning. Here they were going through the motions, putting on set faces before the footlights, but God knows what they were really thinking. This one exclusively preoccupied by a leg which hurt her, that one worried by a dismal rendezvous after work. And still another, thinking: 'I owe a hundred francs.' And the first again: 'It's hurting me.'

Already his old appetite had waned. 'You can give me nothing of what I want,' he thought to himself. Yet so cruel was his loneliness that he needed her terribly.

13

He frightened her, this silent man. When she awoke in the middle of the night and found him sleeping at her side, she had the impression of having been forgotten on some deserted strand.

'Take me in your arms!'

Yet there were moments when waves of tenderness swept over her. But she was troubled by the unknown life bottled up in this body, the unknown dreams under the solid bone of the forehead. Sprawled at an angle across his chest, she could feel the man's respiration rising and falling like a wave, with the restlessness of an ocean crossing. Placing her ear against his skin, she could hear the hard beat of the heart, thumping like a motor, like the pound of a wrecker's hammer. And the silence which ensued each time she uttered a word which pulled him from a dream. She counted the seconds between question and reply, as in a storm between the flash and the thunder – one ... two ... three ... He's already yonder, far beyond those fields. When he closed his eyes, she lifted up his head with her two hands, and found it as heavy as a dead man's, as heavy as a stone. 'What misery, my love!'

Strange fellow-voyager, this! Stretched out side by side without a word. With life flowing through you like a river. And the body, in its dizzying flight, launched on it like a dug-out canoe.

'What time is it?'

Strange voyage indeed – as though one had to chart one's precise position. 'Oh, my lover!' She clung to him, her head thrown back and her hair tangled, as though pulled from the waters. A strand of hair plastered across her brow and her features discomposed, thus woman rises from the sea depths of sleep or love.

'What time is it?'

But why this question? The hours had been passing like provincial railway stations – midnight, one o'clock, two – left behind and lost forever. Something was slipping through one's fingers, as irretrievably as sand. Merely to age is nothing.

'I can picture you quite well with your hair gone white and me sitting quietly beside you, like a friend ...'

Merely to age is nothing. What is wearying is this second that has spoiled, this calm forever deferred and pushed before one, like a stone.

'Tell me what it's like out there?'

'Out there ...?'

But Bernis knew it was impossible. Towns, seas, countries – they were all the same. Occasionally a fleeting glimpse of something surmised more than understood, and which cannot be conveyed.

With his hand he touched this woman's flank, there where the flesh is most defenceless. Woman – the most naked of living flesh, the most luminous and softly glowing. He thought of the mysterious life that animated it, which, like an inner climate, warmed it like a sun. For Bernis she was not soft nor beautiful but warm. Alive, and with this ever beating heart, this wellspring, closed within her body and so different from his own.

He thought of that rapture which, for a few fleeting seconds, had soared within him, flapped its wings like a frenzied bird, and died. And now ...

Now beyond the window the sky was quivering into life. The love-making over, here she was, poor woman, disrobed and uncrowned of man's desire! Banished amid the frozen stars. The landscapes of the heart are so quickly changed ... Thus having crossed the rivers of longing, of tenderness, of fire, here one stands again, pure, cold, detached from one's body, headed like a ship's prow out to sea.

14

The neatly furnished drawing-room was like a station platform, up and down which Bernis paced, killing the last empty hours before his train was due to leave. Pressing his forehead against the windowpane, he watched the crowds flow by. He felt himself left behind by this human flood. Each individual hastening somewhere, bent on some fixed purpose; schemes hatched and unhatched and to which he was not privy. A woman passed, and ten steps further on she was already beyond his ken. Out of sight and out of time. Once this crowd had been the living substance from which your tears and smiles were fed, but for Bernis now it flowed on, like a procession of ghosts.

Part Three

I

In quick succession Europe and Africa made ready for the night, washing away the final storms of the day. Granada's had quieted down, that of Málaga dissolved itself into a shower. Here and there the winds still howled, shaking and uncombing the dishevelled branches.

Having speeded the mail-plane on its way, Toulouse, Barcelona, and Alicante were stacking away their tools, bringing in the planes, and closing the hangars. Málaga, where he was due by daylight, had no need to put out flares. Besides, he would not land there, but fly on low towards Tangier. Today, once more, he would have to cross the Straits at a height of sixty feet, steering by compass and unable to sight the coast of Africa ahead of him.

A powerful west wind was furrowing the sea, whitening the breakers as they lashed against the shore. Each ship, at anchor, rode into the wind, all its rivets straining as on the open sea. In the windless depression, leeward of the soaring Rock of Gibraltar, the rain was pouring down in bucketfuls. To the west the clouds had risen a storey higher. On the opposite shore Tangier was steaming under a dense downpour that was rinsing the city clean. New banks of cumulus were massed on the horizon, although, as he approached Larache, the sky grew clear.

Casablanca was breathing happily under an open sky. The sailboats at their moorings dotted the harbour, like bannered tents after the battle. Where the ploughshare of the storm had passed the sea now showed a calmer surface, over which long wrinkles moved in regular, fan-shaped arcs. The fields, in the evening light, had turned a darker, lake-deep green. Here and there the city's still soaked quarters glistened. In the electro-generating shack the electricians waited idly. Those of Agadir were having dinner in town, having four free hours ahead of them. Those of Port-Étienne, Saint-Louis, and Dakar could go to bed.

At 8 p.m. Málaga beamed this radio message:

Mail-plane passed without landing.

Casablanca now tested its ground landing lights. The red markers cut out a piece of night, a black rectangle. Here and there a lamp was missing, like a tooth. A second switch brought on the searchlights, washing over the centre of the field like milk. The stage was set: only the performer was missing.

A searchlight was hauled into a new position. Its roving beam snagged itself on a still dripping tree, which sparkled briefly like crystal. Then a white shed loomed hugely up, throwing out revolving shadows, only to be blotted out. Finally, descending, the halo struck the ground, respreading its chalk-white hammock for the plane.

'Fine,' said the airfield controller. 'Switch her off!'

He walked back to his office, glanced at the papers that had just come in, and stared absently at the telephone. Rabat should soon be calling. Everything was ready. The mechanics sat around on oildrums and wooden crates.

Agadir was hopelessly disoriented. According to their reckonings, the mail-plane by now had already left Casablanca. A watch was set up for it, just in case. A dozen times the Evening Star was mistaken for its flying light, and the Pole Star too, likewise rising in the north. They waited, before switching on the searchlights, watching for one star too many, for the star they could see wandering across the constellations in vain quest of a place.

The airfield controller was puzzled. Should he send on the plane in his turn? He was afraid the coast might be fogged up as far as the wadi of the Noun, perhaps even as far as Juby; and Juby, notwithstanding repeated radio messages, remained mute. There was no question of launching the France–America mail-plane into a night of cotton-thick clouds. And this Sahara out-post was too secretive for his liking.

Meanwhile, cut off from the world at Juby, we were sending out ship-like signals of distress:

Request news mail-plane, request...

We had stopped answering Cisneros, which had been pestering us with the same questions. Thus, over a distance of six hundred miles, we filled the night with our vain laments.

At 20.50 hours everyone relaxed. Casablanca and Agadir were able to communicate by telephone, and our radios re-established contact. Casablanca was on the air and the message was relayed all the way to Dakar:

Mail-plane will leave 22 hours for Agadir.

Agadir to Juby: mail-plane will reach Agadir midnight thirty stop Can we forward on to you?

Juby to Agadir: Mist. Wait for daylight.

Juby to Cisneros, Port-Étienne, Dakar: Mail-plane stopping night Agadir.

At Casablanca the pilot signed the clearance papers, blinking his eyes under the strong light. A few minutes earlier his eyes had had precious little to feast on; and there were times when Bernis felt lucky to be guided by the white ruin of the waves, there where sea meets earth. Here, in this office, his eyes could feast on a wealth of folders, white papers, and solid furniture. He was in the compact, generous world of matter. Beyond the dark opening of the door was a world emptied of its substance by the night.

His cheeks were red, roughened by the wind, which for ten long hours had massaged his cheeks. Drops of water trickled from his hair. He had emerged from the night like a sewer-worker coming up out of his manhole, with his heavy boots, his leather jacket, and his forehead-plastered hair, blinking like an owl. He stopped writing.

'So you want me to continue?'

The airfield controller leafed through his papers with a frown.

'You'll do as you're told.'

He knew perfectly well that he wouldn't insist on his taking off; and the pilot, for his part, knew he would ask for permission to fly on. But each wanted to prove that the decision was really his.

'Blindfold me and lock me up in a cupboard with a throttle lever in front of me and ask me to fly the crate to Agadir – that's what you're asking me to do.'

He had too much inner life to be at all concerned about an accident to himself – such ideas occur to empty souls – but this cupboard image enchanted him. Certain things are impossible ... but he would bring them off all the same.

The airfield controller opened the door briefly to toss his cigarette stub into the night.

'Look, one can even see some ...'

'Some what?'

'Some stars.'

The pilot flared up.

'I don't care a hoot about your stars! Three of them, that's all there are to see. But it's not to Mars you're sending me, it's to Agadir.'

'The moon will be up in an hour.'

'The moon ... the moon ...'

The moon made him even madder. Had he waited for the moon before learning to fly at night? What did he take him for – a novice?

'All right. Stay.'

The pilot calmed down, pulled out some sandwiches which

had been made up for him the previous day, and chewed them contentedly. He would take off in twenty minutes. The airfield controller smiled. He drummed his fingers on the telephone, knowing that before long he would be announcing the take-off.

Now that everything was settled, there was a kind of void. It was as though time had suddenly stopped. The pilot sat hunched forward in his chair, his grease-blackened hands between his knees. His eyes were focused on a point midway between himself and the wall. The airfield controller, half turned in his chair, had his mouth slightly open, as though he were waiting for some secret signal. The typist yawned, rested her chin on her clenched fist, and felt sleep rising within her. The seconds trickled by, like sand funnelling through an hourglass. Then a distant cry jogged the mechanism into action. The airfield controller raised a finger. The pilot smiled, drew himself up, and took a breath of new air.

'Well, good-bye.'

Thus it is, sometimes, when a film strip snaps. A deadly inertia, like a fainting fit, descends on everything . . . then miraculously, it flickers back to life.

At first he had less the impression of taking off than of shutting himself up in a cold and clammy cave, surf-pounded by the engine's roar. Then of casting off with little to shore him up. By day the round rump of a hill, the curve of a bay, the blue sky above construct a world which holds you; but Bernis now found himself outside of everything, in a world still forming and where the elements were blurred. The plain slid softly back, carrying off the last towns – Mazagan, Safi, Mogador – their lights signalling to him like portholes from below. Then the last farmhouses glimmered, the earth's last mastlights, and suddenly he was blind.

'Back into the broth!' he thought.

Keeping a sharp eye on his altimeter and artificial horizon

gauge, he deliberately lost altitude to emerge from the cloud. His sight was dazzled by the red glow of a lamp on his instrument panel: he turned it off.

'Thank Heaven, I'm out of it. But I still can't see a thing.'

The first summits of the Little Atlas range were drifting by, silent and invisible like half-sunk icebergs. He could feel them looming up under his left shoulder.

'Don't like it one bit!'

He glanced back. A mechanic, his only passenger, was reading a book by the light of a torch, propped on his knees. All Bernis could see emerging from the cockpit was a bent head with upended shadows; it looked odd, lit up from inside, like a lantern. 'Hey!' he shouted, but his voice was lost in the slipstream. He banged his fist against the fuselage, but the man went on reading, silhouetted in his own light; his face, when he turned the page, looked tense. 'Hey!' shouted Bernis once more. Just two arms' lengths away, the man was inaccessible. Abandoning his attempt to converse with him, Bernis turned and faced into the darkness once again.

'I must be approaching Cape Guir, but I'll be damned if I can find it ... Don't like the look of it ...' He reflected for a moment. 'I must be too far out to sea.'

He corrected his course by compass. He had a curious feeling of being pushed towards the open sea to the right of him, as though mounted on a road-shy horse, as though the mountains to his left were shoving him aside.

'It must be raining.'

He put out his hand and felt the raindrops peppering it.

'I'll swing back in towards the coast in twenty minutes' time. It will then be flat land and less risky.'

But suddenly everything cleared! Swept clean of clouds, the sky glittered with new-washed stars. And here came the moon, that best of lamps! The airfield of Agadir lit up in three stages, like a neon poster.

'To hell with your lights! I've got the moon.'

2

Dawn at Cape Juby raised the curtain, to reveal a stage which seemed to me empty. Scenery without shade or perspective. This never-moving dune, this Spanish fort, this desert. Missing was that faint movement which, even in calm weather, is the joy of prairie-lands and seas. The camel-riding nomads could see the texture of the sand change with the slow pace of their caravans; each evening they could pitch their tents on virgin soil. I too could have felt this immensity of the desert had I but been able to move; but the immutable landscape in front of me was as mind-numbing as a colour print.

Two hundred miles farther on there was another well, just like this one. Seemingly it was the same well, the same sand, the same hummocks which rose around it. But out there the fabric of things was new. Renewed, as with each passing second, is the spray of the sea. At the second well I would have felt my solitude, and at the next one tasted the true mystery of the lawless hinterland.

Another bleak day was ending, totally unfurnished with events. We were victims of the solar cycle. For a few hours a naked earth exposed its belly to the sun. Here words gradually lost the guarantee they were assured by our humanity, crumbling slowly into dust. Even the most emotion-charged words – like 'tenderness' and 'love' – provided no ballast in our hearts.

*

If you left Agadir at five, you should have landed by now.

'If he left Agadir at five, he should by now have landed.'

'Yes, old man, yes ... but the wind's from the south east.'

The sky is yellow. In a few hours the wind will upset a

desert which the north wind has been modelling for months. Days of disorder will follow: struck from behind, the dunes will splay out their sand in long tresses, each winding itself down to rebuild further on.

We listen. No. That's the sea.

A mail-plane on its way, that's all. Between Agadir and Cape Juby, over these unexplored and untamed wastes, a friend is both somewhere and nowhere. But by and by in our skies a steady lodestar will seem to rise.

'Left Agadir at five...'

There's a vague hint of trouble. A mail-plane in distress is at first no more than a prolonged suspense, discussions which heat up and explode. With time growing ever longer, like a shadow, and which one does one's best to fill with trivial words and gestures. Then suddenly a fist comes down on the table with a 'For God's sake! It's ten o'clock!' which brings everybody to his feet. A fellow flyer is down, among the Moors!

The radio operator is communicating with Las Palmas. The diesel engine is puffing noisily, the dynamo purring like a turbine. His eyes are glued to the ammeter, where the slightest discharge is registered.

I stand, waiting, by his side. Half turning, he offers me his left hand, while his right continues its tapping.

'What?' he shouts.

I hadn't spoken. Twenty seconds pass. He shouts another phrase, which I don't catch. 'Ah yes?' Around me everything sparkles. A ray of sunshine filters through the half opened shutters; the diesel engine's piston-rods emit wet flashes, churning the dense sunlight with their greasy arms.

The operator wheels about at last and removes his headphone. The engine coughs and stops. In the sudden silence I catch the last words of a phrase shouted at me as though I were a hundred yards away.

'... couldn't care less!'

'Who?'

'They.'

'Ah, I see. Can you get Agadir?'

'It's not yet relay time.'

'Try anyway.'

I scribble a message on the writing pad.

Mail-plane not arrived. Was take-off delayed stop confirm departure hour.

'Here. Send this out.'

'O.K. I'll call them.'

The din starts up again.

'Well?'

'... on!'

He must have meant 'Hang on!' I think. Who's piloting the mail-plane, I wonder. Is it you, Jacques Bernis, now straying out of time, out of space?

The operator switches off the generator, connects a plug, and adjusts his headphone. He taps his pencil on the tabletop, glances at the clock, and yawns.

'Crash-landed ... why?'

'How the devil should I know?'

'Yes, of course. Ah ... nothing. Agadir didn't hear us.'

'You'll try again?'

'I'll try again.'

The engine starts up once more.

Agadir is still silent. We're now listening for its voice. If it starts speaking to another station, we'll break in on the conversation.

I sit down. Having nothing else to do, I pick up an earphone and stumble into an aviary full of twittering birds. Some short, some long, certain trills too rapid – I have trouble deciphering this mode of speech, but what a host of voices are here revealed filling a sky I'd fancied empty.

Three stations were on the air at once. One of them signs off, whereupon another gets into the act.

'That? ... That's Bordeaux, on the automatic.'

There's the same repeated syllable, high-pitched, far-off, insistent. Then a deeper, slower voice breaks in.

'And that?'

'Dakar.'

Now a plaintive tone. The voice stops, resumes, stops and starts up again.

'... Barcelona ... calling London ... but no reply from London.'

Somewhere very faintly in the distance Saint-Assise is murmuring in undertones. What a mass gathering in the depths of the Sahara! All Europe is present, its bird-voiced capitals exchanging cryptic secrets.

A near-by clamour suddenly erupts. A switch plunges the voices into silence.

'Was that Agadir?'

'Yes, Agadir.'

The operator, his eyes for some reason still fixed on the clock, raps out his call.

'Has he heard?'

'No. But he's talking to Casablanca. We'll soon know.'

We are eavesdropping on angels' secrets. The pencil hovers, then comes down on the pad, nailing down a letter, then another, then all of a sudden ten. The words take shape, begin to bloom.

Note for Casablanca ...

Damn it! Tenerife drowns out Agadir! Its huge voice fills the echoing earphones. Then suddenly silence.

'... I landed six thirty left again at ...'

There's Tenerife, that gate-crasher, butting in again. But I've heard what I wanted. At six-thirty the mail-plane returned to Agadir.

'Ground-fog? Engine trouble?'

'... couldn't have left before seven. So not overdue.'

'Thanks.'

3

Now, Jacques Bernis, while I await your coming, I shall say something of the man you are. Yesterday the radio pick-ups enabled us to locate your exact position, and today you will soon be stopping over for the scheduled twenty minutes. I shall open a tin of canned food and uncork a bottle of wine; you won't talk of love or death, or of any of life's real problems, but only of the force and direction of the wind, of the state of the sky, of your motor. You will chuckle over a mechanic's pithy phrase and grumble about the heat – just like the rest of us.

I shall tell of the voyage upon which you are embarked, and why, behind a screen of superficial similarities, your steps in life are not the same as ours.

We are both sprung from the same childhood. Whenever I think back on it, there rises up before my mind the vision of that old, crumbling, ivy-covered wall. We were bold children. 'What are you scared of? Push open the door.'

Yes, an old, crumbling, ivy-covered wall. Dried up, scorched, and seared with sunlight, hardened to a crisp in the oven of slow time. Through the leaves the lizards rustled, those 'snakes' as we called them, for already our spirits were captivated by the image of flight, of death. On this side each stone was warm, rounded and incubated like an egg. Each clod of earth, each twig was stripped of all mystery by the sun. On this side of the wall summer, in all its plentitude, reigned over the countryside. We could see the church steeple, hear a thresher working. The blue of the sky filled every nook and cranny. The peasants were scything their wheatfields, the *curé* spraying his vines, the grown-ups in the salon were playing bridge. We had a name for those who, for sixty years or more and from birth to death, had worked this soil, had taken this sun, these wheatfields, this property into custody: these living generations we called 'The Watch'. For we liked to think of oursèlves as a sea-girt isle, hemmed in between two perilous oceans, the past and the future.

'Turn the key...'

We children were forbidden to open the little green door, whose paint had faded like a timbered hull, or to touch the massive lock, rusted by the years like an old sea anchor. Doubtless it was because the open cistern was dangerous, and there was the ever lurking dread of a child drowning in its slimy waters. Behind this door, we used to say to ourselves, was a water which had lain dormant for a thousand years and of which we thought every time we heard speak of 'dead waters'. Tiny round leaves had spread a solid tissue across it, and the stones we threw into it made holes.

How blissfully cool it was beneath those old, heavy branches, which bore the brunt of the sunlight. Never had a ray yellowed the tender grass of the embankment nor touched its velvet moss. Each pebble we threw out began its course, like a star – for this water, for us, was bottomless.

'Let's sit down...'

There not a sound would reach us. We drank in the freshness of the smell, the coolness of the damp which revived our bodies. We were lost, on the very confines of the world, for already we knew that to travel is above all to change one's skin.

'This is the reverse side of things...'

The reverse side of this self-asserting summer, of these fields and faces which held us captive. For we hated the world that had been imposed upon us. At dinner time we would walk back towards the house, rich with secrets, like those divers of the Indies who have fingered pearls. Just when the sun was sinking and the tablecloth was flushed with rose, we would hear them utter words that galled us:

'The days are getting longer.'

We felt ourselves caught up again by this old roundelay, by a life made up of seasons, holidays, marriages, and deaths. All this vain surface tumult.

Escape, that was the thing! When we were ten we found refuge in the attic's timberwork. Dead birds, old bursting trunks, extraordinary garments – the stage-wings of life. And this treasure we said was hidden, this secret treasure of old houses, so wondrously described in fairy-tales – sapphires, opals, diamonds. This treasure which shone softly. The *raison d'être* of each wall, each beam. Huge beams defending the house against we knew not what. But yes – against time. For time was the arch-enemy. It was kept at bay with traditions, and the cult of the past. Huge beams – but we alone knew that this house was launched like a ship. We alone who visited its holds and bulkheads knew just where she was leaking. We knew the holes in the roof through which the little birds slipped in to die. We knew each crack in the timbering. Downstairs, in the drawing-rooms, the guests conversed and pretty ladies danced. What a deceptive security! No doubt liqueurs were being passed around. By white-gloved butlers in black coats. How fleeting! While we, up there, watched the blue night filter through the crannies in the roof, and saw a star, one solitary star, fall on us through a tiny hole. Decanted for us from the vast expanse of heaven. But it was the star which ails; and hastily we turned away, fearful of the star that brings the kiss of death.

Often we would jump with fright – over the obscure travail of these veterans. The beams would creak, as though split by the treasure, and at each sound we probed the wood. A giant pod getting ready to yield its grain. A time-worn husk beneath which, we were certain, something else lay hidden – be it no more than that star, that small hard diamond. One day we would sally forth – northwards, southwards, or into ourselves – in quest of it. Ah yes, escape!

The sleep-producing star moved out from behind the slate that had been masking it, with the sureness of a sign. We would then go down to our room, ready to embark on the long voyage of half-sleep with a knowledge of a world where the mysterious stone sinks endlessly through the waters, like those tentacles of light which plunge through space for a thousand years to reach us; where a house which creaks and labours in the wind is threatened like a ship, and where one by one all things burst, under the obscure sap-thrust of the treasure.

*

'Have a seat. I thought you'd had a breakdown. Have a drink. I thought you'd crash-landed in the desert, and I was about to take off to look for you. Look, the plane's already out there and ready. The Aït-Oussa have attacked the Izarguin. I was afraid you'd landed in the middle of the rumpus. Drink. What would you like to eat?'

'I must be off.'

'You've still got five minutes. Now tell me – what happened with Geneviève? Why are you smiling?'

'Oh, nothing. Just now, in the cockpit, I was reminded of an old song. Suddenly I felt so young ...'

'And Geneviève?'

'I don't know. I must be off.'

'Jacques, answer me. Did you see her again?'

'Yes ...' He hesitated. 'On the way down to Toulouse I made a detour to see her once more ...'

And Jacques Bernis told me the story.

4

It was less a small provincial station than a hidden door, opening on to the countryside. A placid ticket-collector nodded to him as he made to pass through and out on to the bright, dust-white road, bordered by clumps of sweet briar and a gurgling brook. The station-master was tending the roses, the solitary porter pretending to push an empty trolley. Beneath their separate disguises three watchmen stood guard over a secret world.

The ticket-collector thumbed Bernis' ticket.

'You're on your way from Paris to Toulouse. Why are you getting off here?'

'I'll go on by the next train.'

The ticket-collector looked him over. He hesitated to grant him access – not to a road, a stream, or some sweet briar, but to that realm which, since Merlin, the blessed have learned to enter behind the veil of appearances. Bernis must have seemed to possess the three virtues required of such excursions since the days of Orpheus: courage, youth, and love . . .

'Go ahead,' he said.

The express trains tore through this station, which stood there like some piece of make-believe, as artificial-looking as one of those eerie little bars where everything is bogus – the waiters, the musicians, the barman. Already, in the puffing local, Bernis could feel his life slow down and change. Now, seated next to this peasant on his cart, he was further removed from us than ever. He was plunging deeper into mystery. The peasant, whose ageless face had worn the same wrinkles since he was thirty, pointed to a field: "Coming up fast, there!"

What invisible haste – for us men – this surge of the wheat towards the sun!

Bernis felt us to be even more remote, more restless, more unhappy when the peasant pointed towards a wall. ' 'Twas my grandfather's granddad built that!'

Already he had reached an everlasting wall, an everlasting tree. It meant that they were nigh.

'Here's the estate. Should I wait for you?'

A legendary realm, asleep beneath the waters – it was here that Bernis was to spend a hundred years while ageing but an hour. That same evening the farm-cart, the little local, the express train would make possible that zig-zag escape which brings us back from the world of Orpheus and the Sleeping Beauty. He would look like any other traveller bound for Toulouse, his white cheek pressed against the window-pane. But in the depths of his heart would be buried a memory impossible to describe, a memory 'the colour of the moon', as 'sickly-hued as time'.

Strange visit, indeed! Not a voice to be heard, no greetings of surprise. His footsteps sounded dully on the road. As in the past he jumped the hedge. Tufts of grass had invaded the driveway, but otherwise there had been no change. The house stood out whitely among the trees, impossibly remote, as in a dream. A mere stone's throw from the goal, was this perchance a mirage? He walked up the flag-stoned steps of the entrance. Each stone the fruit of necessity, child of an easeful harmony of line. 'Nothing here is fake . . .'

The hallway was dark. A white hat lay on a chair – was it hers? What a delightful disorder! Not a slovenly disorder, but the meaningful disorder that denotes a presence. The chair, barely stirred, still bespoke the movement: a hand had pressed against the table to help the sitter rise – he could picture the gesture. On the table an open book – left by whom? And why? Perhaps its last sentence was still echoing in the reader's head.

Bernis smiled, thinking of the myriad tiny tasks and worries a household involves. Day in, day out, its inmates had to face the self-same needs, right the same disorders. How trivial – to the foreign, to the wanderer's eye – were the flare-ups and domestic dramas. 'Still,' he thought, 'each evening here was like the finished cycle of a year. Tomorrow ... meant beginning life anew, heading for evening. One's cares were banished. The blinds were drawn, the books neatly stacked, the fire-screens all in place. The rest one earned here could have been eternal, it had something of its savour. But *my* nights are no more than truces ...'

He sat down without a sound. He didn't dare reveal his presence: all seemed so calm, so still. A single sunbeam filtered through the carefully lowered blind. 'A rip,' thought Bernis. 'Here old age creeps up on one unawares.'

'What am I going to discover?' he wondered. A footstep in the next room cast its spell over the house. The quiet footsteps of a nun, arranging the altar flowers. 'What tiny task is being attended to? My life is as tense as a drama. Here, what space, what room to breathe there is between one's every movement, between one's every thought!'

He peered through the window at the countryside. It lay stretched out before him, with long leagues of country roads over which one went to pray, to hunt, to post a letter. In the distance a thresher was purring: he had to strain his ears to hear it – like an anxious audience, straining to catch an actor's failing voice.

He heard the footsteps again. 'They must be dusting the knick-knacks, behind their glass panels. Each century, as it ebbs, leaves its sea-shells behind it.'

Then Bernis heard voices.

'Do you think she'll last out the week? The doctor ...'

The footsteps receded. Bernis was aghast. Who, then, was going to die? His heart sank. But the white hat ... the open book? Such solid signs of life ...

He could hear them speaking again. Voices full of love, but oh so calm! Death had taken up its seat beneath this roof, and they knew enough to greet it as an old acquaintance, rather than try to hide it from their sight. They avoided high-flown phrases. 'How simple it all is,' thought Bernis. 'Living, rearranging the *bric-à-brac*, dying . . .'

'Did you pick the flowers for the drawing-room?'

'Yes.'

They spoke in undertones, in hushed but level voices. They spoke of a thousand trivialities, only faintly shadowed by the imminence of death. There was a short laugh, which died away as suddenly. A shallow laugh, unsuppressed by a theatrical sense of dignity.

'Don't go up,' said the voice. 'She's sleeping.'

Privy to unexpected intimacies, Bernis found himself posted in the very heart of sorrow. He was afraid of being found out. A stranger's presence suffices to unleash a less diffident form of sorrow; forced to express the unstated, they would exclaim : 'But you who knew her, who loved her . . .' And he would have to raise the dying woman in all her grace upon a pedestal. It was more than he could bear.

Yet he had a right to this intimacy . . . 'for I loved her.'

He felt a burning need to see her once again. Stealthily he climbed the stairs and opened the door to her room. It was full of summer radiance : the walls were bright and the bed white. Daylight streamed in through the open window. A church clock in the distance sounded the hour with a slow, peaceful chime, marking the beat a healthy, unfevered heart should have. She was asleep. A glorious midsummer sleep!

'She's going to die . . . He tiptoed across the polished floor, whose varnish mirrored the sun. He was amazed by the sense of peace he felt. She moaned, and Bernis did not dare come closer. He felt a mighty presence everywhere. The soul of a sick person fills the room, until the room is like a wound. One dares not brush up against a table, take a step.

There was not a sound – save for a few buzzing flies. A far-off cry propounded its enigma. A wave of fresh air wafted softly into the room. 'It's evening already.' Bernis thought of the shutters that would be closed, of the lamp that would be lit. Soon it would be night, which would obsess her with the prospect of another lap to be covered. The feeble night-lamp would glow like a mirage, and the objects at whose unmoving shadows one stared for twelve hours at a stretch would imprint themselves on the mind, like a leaden weight.

'Who is it?' she asked.

Bernis moved closer. A wave of tenderness and pity rose to his lips. Oh, to be able to help her, take her in his arms, fill her with his strength!

'Jacques . . .' She stared at him. 'Jacques . . .' From the depths of her thoughts she seemed to be dredging him. It wasn't his shoulder but her memories that she was groping for. She clung to his sleeve like a drowning person clutching, not a presence, nor a foothold, but an image.

She stared at him, and as she did so bit by bit he began to seem a stranger. She did not recognize this look, nor that wrinkle. She squeezed his fingers in a mute appeal, but he could not help her. He was not the friend she carried within her. Already wearied by his presence, she pushed back his hand and turned away her head.

He was light years removed from her.

He fled without a sound, crossing the hallway once again. He was returning from a lengthy voyage, a chaotic voyage he only dimly recalled. Did he grieve? Was he sad? He stopped. The evening was seeping in like water into a leaking hold; the curios had lost their lustre. Pressing his forehead to the window-pane, he saw the shadows under the lindens lengthen, merge, and spread their night over the lawn. The lights sprang up in a distant village – a tiny handful of lights he could have cupped in both his palms. The distance had vanished; and by stretching out his arm he could have touched the hillside with his finger. The voices in the house were hushed: everything was now in order. He did not move. He recalled other evenings similar to this one. One rose to one's feet, as heavy as a deep-sea diver. The woman's face was closed, and suddenly one feared the future, death.

He walked outside. He turned round anxiously, hoping to be surprised and summoned. His heart would have melted from sadness and joy. But nothing happened. There was nothing to hold him back. He slipped effortlessly through the trees and jumped the hedge. The roadway was hard. It was all over. Never would he return.

5

Before taking off, Bernis summed up the story.

'I tried, you see, to drag Geneviève away into a world of my own. But everything I showed her turned drab and grey. That first night was of a nameless depth, and we were unable to cross it. I had to give her back her house, her life, her soul. One by one all the poplars of the highway. The closer we drew to Paris on that return trip, the less thick was the distance between the world and ourselves. It was as if I had been trying to drag her down beneath the sea. When, later, I sought to join her, I managed to approach and touch her. There was no space between us: there was more. I don't know how to put it – a thousand years. One is always so remote from another person's life. She clung to her white sheets, her summer, her "realities", and I could not tear her from them . . . Now let me leave.'

Whither are you now bound in search of the treasure, O diver of the Indies who has fingered pearls but not known how to bring them to the surface? This desert on which I walk, I who am pegged to this earth like a leaden weight, is not likely to yield me anything. But for you, my magician, it is but a veil of sand, an appearance . . .

'Jacques, it's time to leave.'

6

Solidly ensconced in his cockpit, Bernis sank into a reverie. The earth from so high up seemed motionless. The yellow sands of the Sahara curbed the blue sea like an interminable pavement. With a practised hand he halted the coastline which was drifting off to starboard, brought it back towards him in line with his motor. With each curve in the African shoreline he softly banked his plane. Dakar was still twelve hundred miles away.

Before him lay the dazzling whiteness of this lawless wilderness. Here and there the bare rock stood out; elsewhere the wind had swept the sand into serried dunes. His plane was caught in the immobile air, as in a paste. It neither pitched nor rolled, and from this height even the landscape seemed becalmed. Hugged by the wind, the plane droned on. Port-Étienne, the first port-of-call, was not inscribed in space but time. Bernis glanced at his watch. Still six hours of immobility and silence, and then he would climb down from the plane, as from a chrysalis, into a brand new world.

Bernis gazed at the watch which made this miracle possible. Then he looked at the motionless needle of his r.p.m. gauge. If the needle quit its dial figure, if the engine broke down and yielded him up to the mercy of the sand, then these times and distances would take on a new meaning he now could scarcely imagine. He was travelling in the fourth dimension.

Yet this sense of suffocation was nothing new to him. It's one we have all known. So many fleeting images racing past our eyes when in reality we are captives of only one, as dense and weighty as those dunes, that sunlight, this silence. In this ruin of a world we are but weak creatures, armed with feeble gestures barely strong enough at sundown to put the gazelles to flight. Armed with voices barely able to carry three hundred yards and which can reach no human ear. Sooner or later we have all of us come down on this unknown planet. Here time becomes too vast to fit the cramped rhythm of our lives. In Casablanca we could count the hours with reference to our appointments; each of them transformed us. In the air, half an hour was enough to change the climate, and us too. But here we must count by weeks.

From this plight it was our fellow pilots who rescued us. When we were weak, they pulled us up into the cockpit – with a grip of iron which wrenched us from this world and into theirs.

Thus poised over the vast unknown, Bernis could reflect that he knew little about himself. What qualities would thirst, loneliness, or the cruelty of Moorish tribes bring out in him? With Port-Étienne abruptly banished, more than a month hence. But he thought: 'It's not courage I need.'

Everything remained abstract. When a young pilot ventures to try a loop, it is not solid obstacles, the slightest one of which would crush him, which he tosses over his head, but trees and walls of a dream-like fluidity. Courage . . . courage for Bernis? Yet weighing against his heart he could feel it, each time the engine missed a beat – that unknown impostor, ever ready to move in and take his place.

That cape, and then that gulf have at last given way to neutral territories, vanquished by the unwearying propeller. Yet each point of ground ahead is charged with mysterious menace. Still six hundred miles – to be pulled toward one like a blanket.

Port-Étienne to Cape Juby: mail-plane safely arrived 16h. 30.
Port-Étienne to Saint-Louis: mail-plane took off 16h. 45.

Saint-Louis to Dakar: mail left Port-Étienne 16h. 45 will have it continue by night.

*

The wind is now blowing from the east. Blowing from the centre of the Sahara, with the sand rising in yellow whirlwinds. At dawn a pale, elastic sun unglued itself from the horizon, deformed by the hot haze like a pallid soap bubble. But as it rose towards the zenith it contracted, grew smaller and sharper until it became that burning arrow, that branding-iron one can feel against one's neck.

The wind is from the east. In taking off from Port-Étienne into the calm, almost fresh air one has only to climb three hundred feet to strike this searing lava-flow. The dial needle veers upwards:

Oil temperature: 120.

Water temperature: 110.

It's all a question of reaching six thousand, nine thousand feet. Obviously. Anything to get above this sandstorm. Of course. But five minutes of steep climbing and the ignition and the valves will be completely burned out. And it's easy to say – just climb. In this inelastic air the plane founders, bogs down.

The wind is from the east, and one is blind. The sun is tossed about in these yellow spirals. Its pale dusty face emerges, sears, then disappears. Occasionally there's a glimpse of earth beneath, if one looks straight down. But not always. Am I climbing, diving, banking? How am I to know? I can't seem to rise more than three hundred feet. All right, let's try a little lower.

A river of cool north wind greets one at ground level. That's more like it! One lets one's arm trail from the cockpit – as in a swift canoe one rakes the cool water with one's fingers.

Oil temperature: 110.

Water temperature: 95.

As cool as a river? Comparatively, at any rate. The plane dances, each undulation of the ground boots one upwards. Maddening, this lack of visibility.

But at Cape Timeris the east wind is blowing even at ground level. There's no escaping it. There's a smell of burning rubber – is it the magneto? One of the joints? The r.p.m. gauge flickers, loses ten points. 'Now if you too are going to start acting up!'

Water temperature: 115.

Can't even rise thirty feet. A glance at the dune looming up like a springboard. A glance at the oil-gauge. Hop! up and over – that was the upthrust of the dune. One's now piloting with the stick way back. But not for long. Trying to keep the plane on an even keel is like trying to walk along with an overfilled bowl.

Thirty feet below the tyres Mauretania reels out its sands, its saline deposits, its beaches: a torrent of ballast.

1,520 revolutions per minute.

The first air pocket hits the pilot like a fist. Twenty kilometres up ahead there's a French outpost, the only one. But how to reach it?

Water temperature: 120.

Dunes, rocks, saline depressions are swallowed up, whirled back through the wringer. The contours widen, open, then close. Disaster looms at wheel level. Those black rocks grouped together over there seem to be approaching slowly, then suddenly they spurt, scattering wildly beneath one.

1,430 revolutions per minute.

'If I crack-up . . .' The fuselage burns his fingertip. The radiator spouts puffs of steam. The plane, like an overloaded barge, keeps sinking.

1,400 revolutions per minute.

A foot beneath the wheels the last sands came up to meet him, throwing out ever quicker spadefuls of flying gold. The dune ahead was jumped, revealing the fort beyond. Thank Heaven! Bernis cut the ignition. It was time.

The speeding landscape braked. The world in dusty dissolution settled.

*

A French outpost in the Sahara. An old sergeant welcomed Bernis, laughing with joy as though greeting a brother. Twenty Senegalese presented arms. One white man – a sergeant at least; a lieutenant if he's younger.

'Hallo, Sergeant!'

'Come in, come on in! I'm so glad to see you. I'm from Tunis . . .'

His childhood, his memories, his soul – he poured them out pell-mell to Bernis. One small table, and photos tacked up on the walls.

'Yes, family photos. I haven't even met all of them, but next year I'll go to Tunis. That one? . . . That was my pal's sweetheart. He kept her on his table . . . talked about her all the time. When he died I took the photo and stuck it up there . . . as I didn't have a sweetheart . . .'

'Sergeant, I'm thirsty.'

'Well, taste this. I'm glad I can offer you some wine. I didn't have any for the Captain. Came by five months ago. For a long time after I moped. I wrote asking for a transfer, I was so ashamed . . .

'What do I do with myself? . . . I write letters every night – I don't go to sleep and I've got candles. But when the mail gets here, once every six months, the answers are wrong, so I have to begin all over again.'

Bernis went upstairs with the sergeant, for a smoke on the parapet. How empty the desert looked in the moonlight! What could he be watching from this outpost? Doubtless the stars, the moon . . .

'Are you the sergeant of the stars?'

'Have a smoke. Don't say no. I've got plenty of tobacco. But there was none left for the Captain.'

Bernis soon knew everything about this lieutenant and this captain. He could have rattled off their one failing, their sole virtue: one was a gambler, the other was too kind. He also learned that the last visit the lieutenant had made to an old sergeant lost in the sands was almost like a recollection of love.

'He explained the stars to me . . .'

'Yes,' said Bernis, 'he was entrusting them to your safekeeping.'

It was now his turn to explain them. The sergeant, awed by such distances, thought of Tunis, which is also far away. Shown the North Star, he swore he'd recognize its face, he had only to keep it to his left. And he thought of Tunis, so near by.

'And we're falling towards this group at a vertiginous speed . . .'

The sergeant, to keep from falling, steadied himself against the wall.

'But you know everything!'

'No, Sergeant. I even had a sergeant once who said: "Aren't you ashamed, you coming from a good family with a good education, doing your about-turns so badly?" '

'Oh, that's nothing to be ashamed of. Not easy, they aren't.'

Bernis was being consoled.

'Sergeant, look – a lantern to light your watch!'

He pointed to the moon.

'Do you know this song, Sergeant?

Il pleut, il pleut, bergère . . .'

He hummed the tune.

'Do I know it! It's a song they sing in Tunis.'

'Tell me, Sergeant, how does it go on? I'm trying to remember.'

'Let's see . . .

Rentre tes blancs moutons
Là-bas dans la chaumière . . .'

'Sergeant, now it's coming back to me . . .

Entends sous le feuillage
L'eau qui coule à grand bruit.
Déjà voici l'orage . . .'[1]

'Ah, how true it is!' said the sergeant.

They understood the same things.

'It's daylight, Sergeant, we must get to work.'

'Let's get to work.'

'Hand me the spark-plug spanner.'

'Ah, of course.'

'Now bear down here with the pliers.'

'Just give the order. I'll do it.'

'You see, Sergeant, it was nothing. Now I can take off.'

The sergeant looked at the young god, come from nowhere, and now about to fly off. Who had come down to remind him of a song, of Tunis, of himself. From what paradise, beyond the sands, do such handsome messengers so noiselessly descend?

'Good-bye, Sergeant.'

'Good-bye . . .'

Unconsciously the sergeant moved his lips, little realizing what was going on within him. He had stocked up on six months of love, though he would not have known how to say it.

1. It's raining, pretty shepherdess . . .
Take your white sheep home again
Out of the rain, out of the rain.

Listen, listen, in the woods,
The rain is coming down in floods.
The storm is near, the storm is here.

7

Saint-Louis du Sénégal to Port-Étienne: mail-plane not arrived Saint-Louis stop urgent transmit news.

Port-Étienne to Saint-Louis: no news since take-off 16h. 45 yesterday stop dispatching search party immediately.

Saint-Louis du Sénégal to Port-Étienne: plane 632 leaving Saint-Louis 7h. 25 stop delay your departure till plane reaches Port-Étienne.

*

Port-Étienne to Saint-Louis: plane 632 safely arrived 13h. 40 stop pilot reports nothing seen despite fair visibility stop pilot thinks would have found if mail-plane on normal course stop third pilot needed for search in depth.

Saint-Louis to Port-Étienne: O.K. Instructing accordingly.

Saint-Louis to Juby: no news France-America stop proceed immediately Port-Étienne.

*

At Juby a mechanic came back towards me.

'I've stored the water in the left front locker, put the rations in the right-hand locker. There's a spare wheel and the first-aid kit behind. Ready in ten minutes – O.K.?'

'O.K.'

I pulled over the note-pad and jotted down a few instructions.

'In my absence make out daily accounts. Moors to be paid Monday. Load empty drums on to schooner.'

I rested my elbows on the window-sill. The schooner which brought us fresh water once a month was rocking gently on the waves – a charming sight. It brought a bit of trembling life, of fresh linen to my desert. I felt like Noah, visited on his Ark by the dove.

The plane was ready.

*

Juby to Port-Étienne: plane 236 leaving Juby 14h. 20 for Port-Étienne.

The old caravan route is marked by bleaching bones, a few planes mark our own. 'One more hour and we'll reach the plane of Bojador ...' Skeletons stripped bare by the Moors. So many landmarks.

Six hundred miles of sand, then Port-Étienne: four buildings in the desert.

'We were waiting for you. We're taking off immediately to make the most of the daylight. One will follow the coast, the second twenty kilometres inland, the third fifty. We'll be stopping at the outpost because of nightfall. You're changing planes?'

'Yes. Got a sticking valve.'

A quick shift and we're off.

*

Nothing. It was only a dark rock. I go on combing this wilderness. Each black spot is a flaw which troubles me. But all the sand rolls towards me is a dark rock.

I can no longer see my companions. They are off, somewhere in their corner of the sky, scanning the landscape like patient hawks. I can no longer spy the sea. Poised over a white hot brazier, I can't sight a single living thing. My heart beats faster : that wreckage over there? ...

A dark rock.

My motor – a thundering river on the move. This river on the move envelops and exhausts me.

Often, Bernis, I would see you brooding over your baffling hope. I don't know how to put it. But I'm reminded of that phrase of Nietzsche's you were so fond of: 'My brief, hot, melancholy and blissful summer.'

My eyes are tired from so much searching. Black motes dance in front of them. I no longer quite know where I'm going.

*

'So you saw him, Sergeant?'

'He took off at daybreak.'

We sit down in front of the fort. The Senegalese laugh, the sergeant dreams. A luminous but useless twilight.

One of us hazards a suggestion:

'If the plane is wrecked . . . you know . . . won't be much to look for . . .'

'Obviously.'

One of us gets up and takes a few steps.

'Bad business . . . Like a cigarette?'

We enter the night: beasts, men, and things.

*

We enter the night, with a glowing cigarette for navigation light, and the world recovers its real dimensions. The caravans grow old seeking to reach Port-Étienne. Saint-Louis du Sénégal lies on the distant fringe of dreamland. This desert, a while back, was a sand bereft of mystery. There were townships just over the horizon, and a sergeant armed for patience, silence, and solitude, felt the vanity of such virtues. But the wail of a hyena brings the sand to life, an animal cry recreates the mystery, something is born, flees, is born again . . .

Up there the stars serve as the measure of true distances. The simple life, one's abiding love, the girlfriend we think we cherish – the North Star is once more there to light the way.

But the Southern Cross lights up a treasure.

*

Towards three in the morning our wool blankets feel thin, transparent – 'tis the malediction of the moon! I wake up frozen and go up to have a smoke on the parapet. One cigarette, then another. This way it will soon be dawn.

This little outpost under the moonlight is like a smooth-water port. The stars are massed for the help of navigators. The compasses on our three planes are dutifully aimed towards the north. And yet . . .

Was it here that your feet last trod the solid earth? Here ends the tangible world. This little fort is like a wharf. A threshold opening on to this moonlight, where nothing is quite real.

What a marvellous night! Where are you, Jacques Bernis? Here perhaps, or there? Already, how light your presence seems! And round about me this Sahara! Unmarked save here and there by the antelope's wild leap, so little burdened that its heaviest fold can scarcely retain the light imprint of a child.

*

The sergeant came up to join me.

'Good evening, Sir.'

'Good evening, Sergeant.'

He listens. Nothing. A silence, Bernis, made of your silence.

'A cigarette?'

'Yes, thank you.'

The sergeant chews his cigarette.

'Sergeant, tomorrow I'll find my friend. Where do you think he is?'

The sergeant, with a knowing gesture, sweeps his arm over the entire horizon.

A lost child fills the desert.

One day, Bernis, you made me this confession: 'I've liked a life I've never really understood, a life that wasn't completely faithful. I don't even know what I really wanted: it was a faint yearning . . .'

One day, Bernis, you said: 'What I surmised lay behind everything. I had the impression that with a little effort I would understand, I would finally know the truth and carry it away. Now I am leaving, troubled by the presence of a friend I was unable to bring to the surface . . .'

Somewhere, I sense, a ship is foundering. Somewhere, I sense, a child is being bedded down to rest. Somewhere, I sense, this great fluttering of sails, of masts, and hope is slipping inexorably beneath the waves.

*

Dawn. A raucous clamour of Moorish voices. Their camels squat down on the sand, half dead of fatigue. Secretly stolen down from the north, a *rezzou* of three hundred rifles, we are informed, has suddenly appeared some distance to the east and massacred a caravan.

And what if we searched in the direction of the *rezzou*?

'Let's spread out fanwise, shall we? The centre plane will head due east.'

We set off into the teeth of the simoon. A hundred and fifty feet up and it is already drying us out like a vacuum cleaner.

*

My friend, so it was here the treasure . . . which you sought?

Upon this dune last night you lay, your arms spread out as you faced the dark blue gulf, your eyes fixed on those villages of stars. How lightly then your body weighed!

How many moorings you cast off as you flew south, Bernis, my airy one; you who had but one friend left – frail thread of gossamer that linked you to the world.

Tonight, blithe spirit, you weighed even less. Suddenly you

were seized with vertigo. High in the zenith, in the most vertical of stars, the treasure glimmered briefly and was gone!

That one frail thread, my friendship, could not hold you back. Unfaithful shepherd, I must have lain me down and slept.

*

Saint-Louis du Sénégal to Toulouse: France–America located east Timeris stop Bullet holes in controls stop Enemy forces in vicinity stop Pilot killed plane smashed mail intact stop Proceeding to Dakar.

8

Dakar to Toulouse: mail arrived safely Dakar Stop.

Night Flight

Preface

The problem confronting the aerial navigation companies was how to compete in speed with other means of transport. Rivière, that admirable figure of a leader, explains it in this book: 'For us it's a matter of life and death, since we lose at night the lead we gain each day on the railways and steamships.' This night service, much criticized at first but subsequently admitted and made current practice once the initial risks were taken, was still at the time of this narrative a hazardous undertaking. To the impalpable perils of the airways, so fraught with surprises, is here added the perfidious mystery of the night. Great though the risks still are, I hasten to add that they are diminishing with each passing day, each new trip facilitating and improving the prospects of the next. But for aviation, as for the exploration of uncharted lands, there was a first heroic age, and *Night Flight*, which depicts the tragic adventure of one of these pioneers of the air, has the natural ring of an epic.

I like Saint-Exupéry's first book, but I like this one much more. In *Southern Mail* the airman's reminiscences, noted with a striking precision, were linked with a sentimental intrigue which brought the hero closer to us. So sensitive to tenderness, how human, we felt, how vulnerable he was! The hero of *Night Flight*, though anything but dehumanized, rises to a superhuman virtue. What I like most in this stirring story is, I think, its nobility. We are all too familiar with men's weaknesses, renunciations, and backslidings, and contemporary literature has been only too assiduous in denouncing them; but what we needed to have shown to us was above all this surpassing of oneself which can be obtained through sheer force of will.

Even more striking than the figure of the flyer is, in my opinion, that of Rivière, his boss. The latter does not act himself; he prods others into action, imbuing his pilots with his own virtues, exacting the utmost out of them, and forcing them to deeds of prowess. His implacable determination tolerates no flinching, and the slightest lapse is punished by him. His severity might at first sight seem inhuman and excessive. But it is to his imperfections that it applies, and not to the man himself, whom Rivière seeks to mould. In his portrayal of him we sense the fullness of the author's admiration. I am particularly grateful to him for bringing out a paradoxical truth which seems to me of considerable psychological importance: that man's happiness lies not in freedom but in the acceptance of a duty. Each character in this book is ardently, wholeheartedly devoted to what he *should* do, to that perilous task in the sole accomplishment of which he will find the repose of happiness. And it is clear enough that Rivière is anything but insensitive (nothing is more touching than the visit he receives from the lost pilot's wife) and that he needs as much courage to issue orders as his pilots to carry them out.

'To make oneself loved,' he says, 'it's enough to show pity. I show scant pity, or I hide it . . . Sometimes I'm surprised by my power.' And again: 'Love the men whom you command; but without telling them.'

Rivière too is driven by a sense of duty – 'the obscure sense of a duty greater than that of love'. By the idea that man is not an end in himself, but that he subordinates and sacrifices himself to something that dominates him and derives its substance from him. It thus gratifies me to find here that 'obscure feeling' which caused my Prometheus to remark paradoxically: 'I don't like man, I like that which devours him.' This is the source of all heroism. 'We act, Rivière thought, as though there were something exceeding human life in value . . . But what?' Or again: 'Perhaps there is something else, something more lasting to be saved; perhaps it is to save this part of man that Rivière was working.' We may be sure of it.

At a time when the notion of heroism seems to be receding from the army, since manly virtues may find no valid employment in the wars of tomorrow whose horrors our scientists have been foretelling, is it not in the field of aviation that we can see courage most admirably and usefully deployed? Rashness ceases to be such when harnessed to the establishment of a service. The pilot who repeatedly risks his life has some right to smile at our everyday notion of 'courage'. I trust that Saint-Exupéry will forgive me for quoting from a letter, written already long ago at a time when he was flying over Mauretania carrying the Casablanca-Dakar mail.

'I've no idea when I'll be coming home, I've been kept so busy these past months – searches for lost companions; the rescuing of planes crash-landed in dissident territory, not to mention occasional mail-flights to Dakar.

'I've just pulled off a minor exploit – spent two days and nights with eleven Moors and a mechanic, to rescue a plane. All sorts of alarms, some serious, some not. For the first time I heard bullets whining over my head. I now know at last how I am under such conditions – far calmer than the Moors. But I also understood something that had always puzzled me: why Plato (or Aristotle?) places courage on the lowest rung of the virtues. It's not made up of very pretty feelings: a touch of rage, a tinge of vanity, a lot of stubbornness, and a vulgar sportive thrill. Above all, the exaltation of one's physical strength, though this has really nothing to do with. One folds one's arms across one's open shirt and breathes in deeply. Yes, it's rather pleasant. When it happens at night, one has the added feeling of having committed some huge tomfoolery. Never again shall I be able to admire a man who is only brave.'

By way of epigraph to this quotation I might append an

aphorism taken from Quinton's book (which I am far from unreservedly approving): 'One hides one's courage as one does one's love.' Or even better: 'Brave men hide their deeds as honest people do their alms. They disguise them or make excuses for them.'

Everything that Saint-Exupéry here relates is based on 'first-hand' experience. Personal confrontation with a recurrent peril gives his book an authentic and inimitable savour. We have had many war stories and imaginary adventures in which the author sometimes displayed a supple talent but which real adventurers or combatants cannot read without smiling. Quite aside from its literary merits, which I much admire, this book has the value of a document; and it is the unusual combination of these two qualities which gives *Night Flight* its exceptional importance.

ANDRÉ GIDE

I

Already, beneath him, the shadowed hills had dug their furrows in the golden evening and the plains grown luminous with long-enduring light. For in these lands the ground is slow to yield its sunset gold, just as in the waning winter the whiteness of the snow persists.

Fabien, the pilot who was flying the Patagonia mail from the extreme south to Buenos Aires, could note the onset of night by the same telltale signs as a harbour : by the calm expanse before him, faintly rippled by lazy clouds. He was entering a vast and happy anchorage.

In this calm he could also have fancied himself, like a shepherd, going for a quiet walk. Thus the shepherds of Patagonia move unhurriedly from one flock to another. He was moving from one city to the next, and the little towns were his sheep. Every two hours he came upon one slaking its thirst by the riverside or browsing off its plain.

Sometimes, after sixty miles of steppes as uninhabited as the sea, he came upon a lonely farm, which seemed to bob backward on its billow of prairie lands, carrying away its cargo of human lives; he then dipped his wings, as though saluting a ship.

*

'San Julián in sight. We'll be landing in ten minutes.'

The radio operator on board transmitted the news to all the airfields of the network. From the Straits of Magellan to Buenos Aires similar airstrips were strung out over more than fifteen hundred miles. But this one was located on the borderland of night – much as in Africa the last conquered hamlet opens on to the unknown.

The radio operator passed up a slip of paper to the pilot.

'There are so many thunderstorms around that my earphones are full of static. Shall we stop the night at San Julián?'

Fabien smiled. The sky was as calm as an aquarium, and all the airfields ahead of them were signalling: 'Clear sky, no wind.'

'We'll go on,' he replied.

Somewhere, the radio operator thought, a few thunderstorms had managed to lodge themselves, like worms inside a piece of fruit. The night would be beautiful yet spoiled, and he felt ill at ease at the thought of entering this shadow that was ripe to rottenness.

*

Fabien felt tired, as he came down towards San Julián, his engine idling. Looming up to meet him came everything that softens the life of men – their houses, their little cafés, the trees lining their promenades. He was like a conqueror in the aftermath of victory who broods over the lands of his empire and discovers the humble happiness of his subjects. Fabien felt the need to lay down his arms, to feel out his heavy aches and cramps – for one is rich also in one's discomforts – and to become here a simple human being able to look out of the window at an unchanging scene. He would gladly have accepted this tiny village. The choice once made, one can content oneself with the hazard of one's existence and learn to love it. Like love, it hems you in. Fabien would have liked to settle down here, enjoying his morsel of eternity; for the little towns in which he tarried but an hour, and the closed gardens behind old walls over which he flew, seemed to him eternal – for lasting independently of him.

The little town now rose towards the plane, opening wide its arms. Fabien thought of all the friendships it contained, the gentle girls, the privacy of white tablecloths, of everything that is slowly domesticated for eternity. Already the village was streaking past his wings, unfolding the mystery of sheltered gardens no longer shielded by their walls. Yet Fabien knew, even as he landed, that he had seen nothing save a few slow men moving quietly among their stones. By virtue of its very immobility this village defended the secrecy of its passions, withheld its soft welcome; and to conquer it he would have had to give up action.

*

When the ten-minute stop-over was ended, Fabien resumed his flight. He turned to look back at San Julián, now a mere handful of lights. The lights became stars, then a twinkling dust which faded into nothingness along with its temptations.

*

'I can no longer see the dials: I'll light up.'

He flicked on the switches, but the red cockpit lamps gave off a glow that was still so pale in the blue light that it scarcely coloured the needles. He passed his fingers in front of a bulb, but they were barely reddened.

Yet the night was rising, like a dark smoke, and already filling the valleys, which could no longer be distinguished from the plains. The villages were lighting up, greeting each other across the dusk like constellations. With a flick of his finger he blinked his wing-lights in answer. The earth was now dotted with luminous appeals, each house now lighting up its star against the immensity of the night, much as a beacon is trained upon the sea. Everything that sheltered human life now sparkled; and Fabien was overjoyed that his entry into the night should this time be slow and beautiful, like an entry into port.

He ducked his head down inside the cockpit. The phosphorescent needles had begun to glow. One after the other he checked the figures and was happy. He felt himself solidly ensconced in this evening sky. He ran a finger along a steel rib and felt the life coursing through it; the metal was not vibrant but alive. The engine's five hundred horse-power had charged the matter with a gentle current, changing its icy deadness into velvet flesh. Once again the pilot in flight experienced neither giddiness nor intoxicating thrill, but only the mysterious travail of living flesh.

He had made a world for himself once more. He moved his arms to feel even more at home, then ran his thumb over the electric circuit diagram. He fingered the various switches, shifted his weight, settled back, and sought to find the position best suited for feeling the oscillations of these five tons of metal which a moving night had shouldered. Groping with his fingers, he pushed the emergency lamp into position, let it go, seized hold of it again after making sure it wouldn't slip, then let go to touch each throttle lever and to assure himself that he could reach them without looking – thus training his fingers for a blind man's world. His fingers having taken stock of everything, he switched on a lamp, decking out his cockpit with precision instruments. Attentive to dial readings, he could now enter the night, like a submarine starting on its dive. There was no trembling, no shaking, no undue vibration; and as his gyroscope, altimeter, and r.p.m. rate remained constant, he stretched his limbs, leaned his head back against the leather seat, and fell into an airborne meditation rich with unfathomable hopes.

*

Now, swallowed up by the night like a watchman, he could see how the night betrays man's secrets: those appeals, those lights, that anxiety. That single star down there in the shadow – a house in isolation. That other star flickering and going out – a house closing the shutters on its love. Or on its boredom. A house that has ceased signalling to the rest of the world. Gathered around their lamp-lit table, those farmers little guessed the true measure of their hopes nor realized how far their yearnings reached in the great night that encompassed them. But Fabien, approaching from six hundred miles away, uncovered them along with the ground-swells that lifted and lowered his breathing plane. Having traversed ten storms, like battlefields, and the moonlit clearings between them, he now picked up these lights, one after another, with a pride of conquest. Down there they thought their lamp was lit for their humble table, but already from fifty miles away one was touched by its desolate appeal, as though they were desperately swinging it, from a deserted island, at the dark immensity of the sea.

2

From south, west, and north the three mail-planes from Patagonia, Chile, and Paraguay were now converging on Buenos Aires. Here their mail-loads were awaited, prior to the departure, around midnight, of the Europe-bound plane.

Three pilots, each behind a cowling as heavy as a river barge, were thus lost in the night. Wrapped in their airborne meditations, they would soon, from their skies of storm or calm, begin their slow descent towards the great city, like rough backwoodsmen descending from their mountains.

On the landing field of Buenos Aires Rivière, who was responsible for the entire network, was pacing up and down. He said nothing, for until the three planes were safely landed, this day for him remained fraught with anxiety. With each passing minute, as the telegrams came in, Rivière felt he was wrenching something from blind fate, he was reducing the area of uncertainty, and pulling his crews out of the night and towards the shore.

A member of the ground crew came up to him with a message from the radio hut:

'Chile mail-plane reports Buenos Aires lights in sight.'

'Fine.'

Rivière would soon hear its welcome drone. Already the

night was yielding up one of its prey – much as the sea, in the ebb and flow of its mysterious currents, deposits on the shore a treasure it has long tossed about. Later he would retrieve the other two. Then his work-day would be finished. Then the exhausted crews could go to bed, replaced by a new shift. Rivière alone would know no rest; for the Europe-bound mail-plane would cause him anxieties in its turn. So it would aways be. Always.

For the first time this veteran battler experienced a surprising lassitude. Never could his planes' arrival bring him that victory which terminates a war and opens an era of joyous peace. Each forward step he took would be followed by a thousand others like it, remaining to be taken. He was oppressed by the numbing weight of this burden he had been carrying, with taut arms, for so long : it was an effort without hope of respite.

'I must be ageing,' he thought. Yes, ageing – if he could no longer find solace in his work. He was surprised to find himself turning over questions he had never stopped to ask – above the melancholic murmur of gentle joys he had consistently pushed aside, like an unsailed ocean. 'Is it then so near?' For years, he realized, he had been postponing for his old age, for 'when I have time for it', everything that softens and sweetens human life. As though one day one really could find the time, as though at the very extremity of one's life one could gain the blessed peace one had imagined. But there was no peace; perhaps not even victory. There was no such thing as a definitive arrival for every mail-plane in the air.

Rivière stopped in front of Leroux, an old foreman who was hard at work. Leroux, too, had been working forty years; a work that had consumed all his strength. When Leroux went home at ten o'clock or midnight, it was not another world that greeted him, it was not an evasion. Rivière smiled, as the man raised his heavy head and pointed to a polished axle : 'The fit was too tight, but I've pared her down a bit.'

Rivière bent down to peer at the steel-blue axle. His work once again absorbed him.

'We must tell the workshops to adjust these pieces more loosely.' He ran his fingers over the area which had seized, then looked at Leroux again. At the sight of those stern wrinkles a strange question rose to his lips and made him smile.

'In your life, Leroux, have you ever been much concerned with love?'

'Love, Monsieur le Directeur ! . . . Huh . . .'

'Like me, you've never had time for it.'

'No, not much . . .'

Rivière listened to his voice, seeking to detect a note of bitterness in the reply. But there was none. Looking back over his life, this man experienced the quiet contentment of the carpenter who has just polished a handsome board. 'There, it's done.'

'That's it,' thought Rivière. 'My life is done.'

Brushing aside the sombre thoughts his fatigue had brought on, he walked towards the hangar; for already he could hear the drone of the plane from Chile.

3

The sound of the distant engine grew steadily denser : a sound that was ripening. The lights were switched on. The red markers winked gaily from the hangar roof, hung like rubies from the radio aerials, and traced out a rectangle on the ground. A gala fiesta !

'Here she comes !'

The plane rolled towards them, already caught in a cross-fire of beams which made it sparkle like a fish. Halted at last in front of the hangar, mechanics and ground crewmen crowded round to unload the mail, but the pilot, Pellerin, did not move.

'Well, and what are you waiting for?'

The pilot, busy with some mysterious task, did not bother to reply. Probably his ears were still full of the noise of the flight. He nodded his head deliberately as he leaned forward to tinker with some unseen object. Finally he turned towards the officials and the crewmen and looked them over gravely, as though they belonged to him. He seemed to be counting, measuring, and weighing them; he had earned them well, he thought, like this festooned hangar and this solid strip of cement, and farther on, the city with its bustle, its women, and its warmth. He held these people in his broad hands, like subjects, since he could touch them, hear them, insult them. For a moment he felt like bawling them out for standing there so quietly, so unimperilled, so full of gaping admiration for the moon; but instead he greeted them nonchalantly:

'... Owe me a drink!'

And he climbed down. He wanted to tell them of his flight:

'If only you knew ...'

But evidently deciding that he had said enough, he walked off to change out of his leather gear.

*

As the chauffeur-driven roadster took him into Buenos Aires, seated next to a taciturn Rivière and a morose inspector, Pellerin suddenly felt dejected. It was fine to pull through like this and to let go with a volley of swearwords as one set foot on solid ground. It made one feel great! But later, when one looked back on it, one began to wonder ...

That struggle with the blizzard, that at least was real, straightforward. But not the curious look things have when they think they are alone. 'It's like a mutiny,' he thought. 'The faces are only a wee shade paler, but everything's completely changed.'

He made an effort to recall the precise sequence of events. He had been flying over the cordillera of the Andes. Beneath their coverlets of snow the mountains slept. The winter snows had spread their peace over this mountain mass, like the passage of the centuries in dead castles. One hundred and twenty miles across, one hundred and twenty miles of thickness – without a man, a breath of life, a movement. Nothing but vertical ridges which one grazed at twenty thousand feet, nothing but gigantic coats of stone dropping sheer, nothing but an awe-inspiring silence.

Then, as he was approaching the peak of Tupungato – he paused – yes, it was there that he had witnessed a miracle.

At first he had noticed nothing, but simply experienced a vague malaise – such as a man feels when, thinking himself alone, he suddenly becomes aware that someone is watching him. Too late and without understanding why, he felt himself ringed by anger. That was all. Yet why this feeling? By what tell-tale sign could he sense it oozing from the rocks, oozing from the snow? For nothing seemed on its way to meet him, no sombre storm was on the march. Yet a different world, so faintly different as to be barely perceptible, was right here emerging from the other. Pellerin looked on with an inexplicable tightening of the heart – at these innocent peaks, those snowy crests which, grown only slightly greyer, were now beginning to live – like a people.

Instinctively his hands tightened their grip on the controls. Something he did not understand was brewing. He steeled his muscles, like a beast about to spring, but there was nothing he could see that wasn't calm. Calm, yes, but charged with a weird power.

Suddenly everything began to sharpen. Crests, peaks grew razor sharp, cutting into the hard wind like bowsprits. And it seemed to him that they were veering and drifting like giant dreadnoughts, taking up their battle stations around him. Then, faintly mingled with the air, came a fine dust which rose, floating softly like a veil, along the snow. He glanced back, to see if, in case of need, there was an avenue of escape behind him, and shuddered: the entire cordillera behind him was now in seething ferment.

'I'm done for!'

From a peak dead ahead of him the snow suddenly flared – the fume of a white volcano. Then from a second peak, slightly to the right. One after another, all the peaks caught fire as though successively touched by some invisible runner. And now, as the first air bumps hit him, the mountains about him began to dance.

Violent action leaves little trace behind it; and of the mighty buffeting which followed he had but a dim recollection. All he could remember was how grimly he had fought it out in the midst of those grey flames.

'A blizzard,' he reflected, 'is nothing. One saves one's skin. But just before – that weird encounter!'

That changing face, that one face in a thousand he was sure he could recognize . . . had fled, and he could no longer say what it was like.

4

Rivière looked at the pilot. When in twenty minutes' time Pellerin climbed out of the car, he would lose himself in the crowd with a feeling of heavy-limbed fatigue. 'I'm worn out . . . What a dog's life!' he might think. To his wife he might admit that 'one's a lot better off here than over the Andes!' Yet everything men cling to most dearly had almost been ripped from him; he had sensed its fragility. He had just lived through several hours behind the *trompe-l'oeil* screen of this deceptive world, without knowing if he would be allowed to regain this city with its lights, if he would be allowed to renew acquaintance with those irksome but dear companions of his youth, his all too human frailties.

'In every crowd,' Rivière thought, 'there are people whom one cannot tell from the rest but who are prodigious messengers. Without their realizing it themselves . . . Unless . . .'

Rivière was wary of certain admirers, those who do not understand the character of adventure, whose enthusiastic exclamations distort its meaning and debase the individual. Pellerin's merit lay in his knowing, better than anyone, what the world is like when it has been glimpsed in a certain light, and in repelling all vulgar displays of approval with a weary disdain. Rivière therefore congratulated him quite simply: 'But how did you manage it?' Liking him all the more for talking shop, for speaking of his flight as a blacksmith speaks of his anvil.

Pellerin began by explaining that his retreat was cut off. He almost apologized for it. 'I was thus left with no choice.' Then everything had been swallowed up, and he had been completely blinded by the snow. He had been saved by some violent updraughts which had lifted him to twenty-two thousand feet. 'I must have been carried straight over the peaks for the entire crossing.' He also spoke of the gyroscope, saying that the position of its air-intake should be altered: the snow clogged it up – 'It frosts up, you see.' Later he had been tossed around by other air currents, and Pellerin did not understand how he could have dropped to ten thousand feet without smashing into something. In reality, he was already flying over the plain. 'I didn't realize it until I suddenly came out into a clear sky.' At which point he had had the impression of emerging from a cave.

'Was it stormy at Mendoza too?'

'No. I landed under a clear sky, and there was no wind. But the storm was hot on my heels.'

He described it because, as he said, 'it was a bit odd, after all.' The top of the storm was lost high up in the snow clouds, while at its base it rolled out over the plain like black lava. One by one it had blotted out the towns. 'Never seen anything like it . . .' He lapsed into silence, gripped by some memory.

Rivière turned to the inspector.

'It's a cyclone from the Pacific, they failed to warn us in time. Anyway, these cyclones never get beyond the Andes.'

The inspector, who knew nothing, agreed – little realizing that contrary to all expectations, this one would carry on towards the east.

*

The inspector seemed to hesitate, turned towards Pellerin, and his Adam's apple moved. But he said nothing, preferring on second thoughts to look straight ahead of him and retain his melancholy dignity.

He had been carrying this melancholy around like a handbag. He had landed the evening before in Argentina, summoned by Rivière on some unspecified assignment; but he felt encumbered as much by his big hands as by his inspectorial dignity. He had no right to admire fantasy or verve; it was his job to admire punctuality. He had no right to have a drink with the others, to call a pilot by his first name, or to risk a pun unless, by some extraordinary coincidence, he happened to bump into another inspector at the same airfield.

'It's difficult,' he thought, 'to be a judge.'

In sober fact he didn't judge, he merely nodded his head. To mask his ignorance, he nodded his head deliberately, whatever came his way. It troubled the consciences of those who had reasons for feeling guilty, and it contributed to the good upkeep of the material. He was not liked, for inspectors are not created for the delights of love but for the drafting of reports. He had given up proposing new methods and technical solutions since the day Rivière had written: 'Inspector Robineau is requested to supply us with reports, not poems. Inspector Robineau will put his talents to good use by stimulating the zeal of the personnel.' Since then he had fastened on human failings as on his daily bread – the mechanic with a fondness for the bottle, the airfield boss who lived it up at night, the pilot who bounced his plane on landing.

Rivière liked to say of him: 'He's not very intelligent, which is why he gives us yeoman service.' A regulation laid down by Rivière afforded him a knowledge of his men; but for Robineau what mattered was a knowledge of the regulations.

'Robineau,' Rivière had said to him one day, 'for all tardy take-offs you must cancel the punctuality bonus.'

'Even when it's no one's fault? Even in case of fog?'

'Even in case of fog.'

Robineau had felt a kind of pride in having a boss who was not afraid to be unjust. Robineau even derived a certain majesty from such an uncompromising power.

'You had the plane take off at 6.15,' he would later repeat to the airfield controllers, 'we can't pay you your bonus.'

'But Monsieur Robineau, at 5.30 one couldn't see ten yards in front of one.'

'Those are the regulations.'

'But Monsieur Robineau, we can't sweep the fog away!'

Robineau withdrew into his mystery. He was part of the management. He alone, among all these nonentities, understood how, in punishing individuals, one improves the weather.

'He doesn't think,' Rivière used to say of him, 'which keeps him from thinking wrong.'

If a pilot damaged a plane, he lost his no-accident bonus.

'And what if his motor gives out over a wood?' Robineau had asked.

'He still loses it over a wood.'

Robineau did not try to argue.

'I regret,' he would later say to the pilots, almost zestfully. 'I even regret it greatly, but you should have had your breakdown somewhere else.'

'But Monsieur Robineau, one can't choose . . .'

'Those are the regulations.'

'Regulations,' thought Rivière, 'are like the rites of a religion which seem absurd but which mould men.' Rivière did not mind whether he appeared just or unjust. Perhaps these words were devoid of meaning for him. The *petit bourgeois* inhabitants of little provincial towns go strolling in the evening around their bandstands, and Rivière thought: 'Being fair or unfair towards them is meaningless; they don't exist.' Man for him was like a lump of wax waiting to be moulded. It was up to him to give a soul to this matter, to imbue it with a will. In bearing down he had no thought of enslaving them; he meant to raise them up above themselves. In punishing for each delay he might be unjust, but on every airfield he was galvanizing a will to punctuality, and thus creating this will. Denying his men a chance to rejoice over cloudy weather, as a pretext for indolence, he kept them on the *qui vive* for the first break, and even the humblest groundcrew worker felt secretly humiliated by the delay. Thus they learned to take advantage of the first chink in the armour. 'There's a break in the north. Be off!' Thanks to Rivière, the cult of the mail took precedence over everything – over a distance of ten thousand miles.

Occasionally Rivière would say: 'These men are happy because they enjoy what they're doing, and they enjoy it because I'm tough.'

Perhaps he made men suffer, but he also afforded them keen joys. 'They must be pushed,' he thought, 'towards a hardy life involving suffering and joy which by itself matters infinitely more.'

As the automobile entered the city, Rivière had himself driven to the Company offices. Robineau, finding himself alone with Pellerin, looked at him and opened his mouth to speak.

5

Now Robineau this evening felt downcast. In contrast to Pellerin the winner, he was made painfully aware of what a grey life was his. Above all, it dawned on him that for all his authority and title of Inspector, he, Robineau, counted for less than this weary fellow who now sat slumped back in one corner of the car with his eyes closed and his hands black with oil. For the first time Robineau was seized with a genuine admiration. He felt the need to say so, and particularly needed to make a friend. His own trip had tired him and the day's rebuffs perhaps made him feel a bit ridiculous. A bare hour or two before he had got mixed up in his figures while checking the fuel stocks, and the very agent he had hoped to catch off guard had finally taken pity and finished them for him. Worse still, he had criticized the installation of a B6 type oil-pump, confusing it with a B4 type oil-pump, and the mechanics had slyly let him rant on for twenty minutes against 'an ignorance for which there's no excuse' and which was quite simply his own.

He also dreaded his hotel room. From Toulouse to Buenos Aires it was inevitably to it that he repaired when the day's work was done. He would close the door behind him, conscious of the secrets to which he had been privy, and pulling out a sheaf of paper from his suitcase, he would begin with deliberate care: 'Report', try out a couple of lines, and then tear everything up. He would have liked to rescue the Company from some mighty peril, but it was not in danger. All he had so far rescued was a propeller-boss, slightly touched by rust. He had slowly run his finger over this rust with a rueful air, in the presence of the airfield controller, whose only comment was: 'Take it up with the previous stop. This plane's only just come in.'

Robineau was losing confidence in his rôle.

To win Pellerin over he hazarded an invitation: 'Would you like to have dinner with me? I could do with a little conversation, and my job's sometimes tiring ...' But to keep his dignity from slipping too far, he hastily rectified: 'I've so many responsibilities.'

His subordinates didn't care to bring Robineau into their private lives. Each thought to himself: 'If he hasn't yet dug up something for his report, he'll dig his teeth into me.'

But Robineau this evening could think only of his physical afflictions: the annoying eczema which plagued his body, his one and only secret, a secret he would have liked to share, to elicit sympathy; for the solace he could not find in pride he was ready to look for in humility. And then there was the mistress, back in France, whom he would regale with descriptions of his inspection tours each time he came home. He thus hoped to dazzle her a little and make her love him, but all it did was get on her nerves. About her too he felt the need to talk.

'Well, will you dine with me?'

Goodnaturedly Pellerin accepted.

6

The secretaries were drowsing in the Buenos Aires offices when Rivière walked in. He had kept on his overcoat and hat, like the eternal traveller he always seemed to be. So spare was he of build and so perfectly did his grey hair and suit adapt themselves to different settings that his presence went almost unperceived. However, a sudden zeal seized hold of the staff. The secretaries began bustling about, the chief clerk leafed hurriedly through the latest papers, the typewriters began to click.

The switchboard operator kept plugging in his leads, jotting down the telegrams in a bulky register. Rivière sat down and read them. The Chile mail-plane's ordeal now over, they recorded one of those uneventful days when everything goes smoothly and each new airfield message is like a victory bulletin. The Patagonia mail-plane was also doing well; it was even ahead of schedule, for the southern winds were pushing it northwards on their mighty tide.

'Hand me the weather reports.'

Each airfield vaunted its fine weather, its transparent sky, its friendly breeze. A golden evening now robed America. Rivière was pleased to find things going so well. Somewhere this mail-plane was now at grips with the perils of the night, but the odds were in its favour.

'All right,' said Rivière, laying down the register.

And he walked out, tireless watchman of the hemisphere, to have a look at what the rest of his staff were doing.

*

He stopped before an open window and gazed out at the night. It contained Buenos Aires, but also, like some huge hull, America. This feeling of immensity did not surprise him. The sky of Santiago de Chile might be a foreign sky, but once the mail-plane was off for Santiago, from one end of the line to the other one lived under the same deep vault. The fishermen of Patagonia could now see the navigation lights of the mail-plane whose message the radio operators were straining to catch in their earphones. The anxiety that preyed upon Rivière when a plane was in flight was the same as that which weighed upon the capitals and provinces, disturbed by an engine's restless drone.

Relieved by this auspicious night, he recalled nights of chaos and confusion, when the plane had seemed dangerously beset and so difficult to succour. Its plaintive calls were received at the Buenos Aires radio hut amid the atmospheric cracklings of thunderstorms. Beneath this sonic landslide the golden vein of the wave-length disappeared. What piercing distress in this plaintive minor key of a mail-plane launched like a blind arrow at night's obstacles!

*

It occurred to Rivière that an inspector's place, when the staff is on night duty, is in the office.

'Send for Robineau,' he said.

Robineau, in his hotel room, was in the process of making a friend of the pilot. He had opened his suitcase in front of him and dragged out a few trivial belongings whereby inspectors prove their kinship with the rest of mankind: some deplorably-styled shirts, a toilet kit, and a woman's photograph which the inspector pinned up on the wall. To Pellerin he thus made the humble confession of his needs, affections, and regrets. A pitiful hoard of treasures which he laid out before the pilot as a token of his wretchedness. It was a moral eczema, a prison which he thus unveiled.

But for Robineau, as for all men, there was a crack in the darkness. And it was with something akin to rapture that he pulled up from the bottom of his suitcase a small, preciously wrapped bag. He fondled it for a long moment without a word. Then removing his hands, he said:

'I brought these back from the Sahara.'

The inspector, in hazarding this confession, blushed. In these blackish pebbles which opened a door on a mysterious world, he had found solace from his setbacks and sentimental misadventures and the grey drudgery of his life.

Blushing even deeper, he added: 'One can find the same in Brazil.'

Amused by the sight of this inspector, who nourished his own mystery of Atlantis, Pellerin gave him a friendly pat on the back, before dutifully inquiring:

'You like geology?'

'I'm mad about it.'

Stones, in his harsh existence, were the only soft things he had ever known.

*

Informed that he was wanted at the office, Robineau felt sad but promptly resumed his dignity.

'I must leave you. Monsieur Rivière needs my assistance for some important decisions.'

When Robineau walked into the office, Rivière had forgotten all about him. He was staring wonderingly at a wall-map on which the Company's network had been traced out in red. The inspector stood waiting for his orders. Finally, after several long minutes, Rivière addressed him, without turning his head.

'What do you think of this map, Robineau?'

Often Rivière would interrupt his meditations by springing a conundrum on his startled visitor.

'That map, Monsieur le Directeur . . .'

The inspector, in reality, had no ideas on the subject. But now, focusing on it with a frown, he inspected the land masses of Europe and America. Rivière, meanwhile, was pursuing his own silent train of thought. 'The outline of this network is beautiful but hard. It's cost us a lot of men, young men too. Here it imposes itself with the self-evidence of a finished structure, but what a host of problems it presents!' For Rivière, however, the goal took precedence over everything.

Robineau, who had been standing beside him looking fixedly at the map, gradually drew himself up. From Rivière, he knew he could expect no pity. He had once made a fumbling effort to obtain it by avowing his physical infirmities, and Rivière had answered with a quip: 'If it keeps you from sleeping, it should stimulate your activity.'

Even then, it was only half a quip. For Rivière liked to say that 'if the insomnia of a musician causes him to create beautiful works, it is a beautiful insomnia.' One day, pointing to Leroux, he had said : 'Look at that ! What beauty there is in the ugliness that repels love ! . . .' Leroux may well have owed his finest qualities to this misfortune, which had forced him to live only for his job.

'Are you a close friend of Pellerin's?'

'Er . . .'

'I'm not holding it against you.'

Rivière faced about and with his eyes fixed on the floor he took a few short steps, with Robineau beside him. A sad smile came to his lips for some reason Robineau could not fathom.

'Only . . . only . . . you are the boss.'

'Yes,' said Robineau.

Every night, thought Rivière, some new action, like a drama, was unfolding in the sky. Any slackening of willpower could entail defeat, and between now and dawn the struggle might be grim.

'You must keep your place.' Rivière weighed his words. 'To-morrow night you may have to order this pilot out on a dangerous flight. He will have to obey.'

'Yes.'

'Upon you depends the life and welfare of men, and of men who are worth more than you . . .' He seemed to hesitate. 'That's a serious matter.'

Still pacing up and down with small neat steps, Rivière let several seconds go by.

'If it's out of a feeling of friendship that they obey you, then you are deceiving them. You yourself have no right to ask a sacrifice of them.'

'No, of course not.'

'And if they think that your friendship will spare them certain unpleasant chores, you are also deceiving them. For they have no choice but to obey. Now sit down there.'

Gently Rivière pushed Robineau towards his office.

'Robineau, I'm going to teach you a lesson. If you feel tired, it's not the job of these men to buck you up. You are the boss. Your weakness is ridiculous. Now write . . .'

'I . . .'

'Write: "Inspector Robineau imposes such and such a penalty on the pilot Pellerin for such and such a motive . . ." It's up to you to find the motive.'

'Monsieur le Directeur!'

'Act as though you understood, Robineau. Love the men you command – but without telling them.'

Robineau, once more, would see to it that the propeller-bosses were zealously scrubbed.

*

A radio message from an emergency landing-strip announced: 'Plane in sight. Plane signals: reduced engine speed, am landing.'

That would almost certainly mean a half hour lost. Rivière felt the irritation the traveller experiences when the express train comes to a halt on the track and the minutes no longer yield their crop of passing plains. The large clock-hand would now traverse an empty space, within whose ample compass so many events might have been fitted. To while away the interval Rivière left his office: the night now seemed empty like a stage without actors. 'A night like this wasted!' he thought, as he stared out of the window. He was irked by this cloudless sky bejewelled with stars and that moon vainly squandering its gold among the twinkling ground-lights of heaven.

*

But once the plane had taken off, the night for Rivière was once more filled with beauty and enchantment. Its loins were now quick with life, and Rivière was its custodian.

'What kind of weather have you?' he had the radio operator ask the crew. Ten seconds passed.

'Very fine.'

Then came the names of several more towns overflown, and for Rivière, in this battle, they had the sound of vanquished cities.

7

An hour later the radio operator of the Patagonia mail-plane felt himself softly heaved up, as by a giant shoulder. He looked about him: heavy clouds were extinguishing the stars. He leaned over and peered down at the earth, looking for the lights of villages, hidden like glow-worms in the fields, but nothing shone in this black grass.

He felt depressed, foreseeing a difficult night – with marches, countermarches, and occupied territories they would have to yield. He didn't understand the pilot's tactics; for a little farther on, it seemed to him, they would butt up against the thickness of the night as against a wall.

Directly in front of them he could now perceive a faint glimmer on the rim of the horizon, the pale glow of a forge. The radio operator tapped Fabien's shoulder, but the pilot did not budge.

The first tremors of the distant storm began hitting the plane. Gently heaving up, its metal mass compressed the radio operator's flesh, then seemed to relax and melt into the night, leaving him for several seconds floating weightlessly. Convulsively he gripped the metal spars on either side. Now that there was nothing more of the world to be seen than the red cockpit lamp, he shuddered at the thought that they were dropping into the heart of the night, helpless and with only a small miner's lamp to guide him. He dared not disturb the pilot to find out what he intended doing; and, his hands gripped around the steel, he leant tensely forward, staring at the dark form ahead of him.

A head and two unmoving shoulders were all that could be seen in the dim light. The pilot's body was a dark mass, slightly humped over to the left, his face turned towards the storm and doubtless washed by its flickering flashes. The radio operator could see nothing of this face : hidden from him were the feelings that were being mustered to deal with the storm – the tight-set lips, the determination, the anger, the elemental exchange taking place between this pale face and those brief flashes in the distance.

Yet he could sense the strength concentrated in that immobile shadow, and he liked it. It was carrying him towards the storm, but it also shielded him. Those hands, gripping the controls, weighed already on the storm as on the neck of a wild beast, but the strong shoulders remained motionless, attesting deep reserves of strength. After all, the radio operator thought to himself, the pilot was responsible. So now, borne like a pillion-rider on this gallop towards the blaze, he relished what the dark form in front of him conjured up in material weight and durability.

To the left, as faint as a flashing beacon, a new fire was kindled. The radio operator reached forward to touch Fabien's shoulder by way of warning, but he saw him slowly turn his head and stare this new enemy in the face for several seconds, then slowly revert to his original position. His shoulders were as motionless as ever, like the back of his head, solidly pressed against the leather pad.

8

Rivière had gone out to stretch his legs a bit and to forget the malaise which kept nagging at him. He who only lived for dramatic action now felt a curious shifting of the drama as it became more personal. Grouped about their bandstands, he reflected, the middle-class inhabitants of little towns lived lives that were outwardly sedate yet sometimes marked by crises – illness, love, bereavements – and who knows? . . . his own malaise was proving similarly instructive. 'It opens windows,' he thought, 'on many things.'

Feeling refreshed, he turned and headed back towards the office. It was almost eleven. Crowds had gathered in front of the cinemas and he had to shoulder his way through them. He raised his eyes towards the stars, glittering faintly above the narrow street, almost obliterated by the bright neon signs, and thought: 'Tonight, with two mail-planes in the air, I am responsible for an entire sky. That star up there is a sign, searching me out and finding me in this crowd. It's why I feel something of a stranger, a bit lonely.'

A musical phrase came back to him, some notes in a sonata he had been listening to the day before with some friends. His friends had not understood it. 'This music bores us and you too, only you won't admit it.'

'Perhaps . . .' he had answered.

Then, as again tonight, he had felt lonely, but he had quickly realized the wealth of such a solitude. The message of this music had reached him, alone among these humdrum folk, with the softness of a secret. So now this star. Above all these shoulders he was being spoken to in a tongue which he alone could hear.

Someone jostled him on the pavement. 'I won't get angry,' he thought. 'I'm like the father of a sick child, walking with short steps in the crowd. Within him he carries the hushed silence of his house.'

He looked at the people around him, seeking to recognize those among them who with little steps were out walking their invention or their love; and he thought of the loneliness of lighthouse-keepers.

*

The silence of the offices pleased him. He walked slowly through them, one after the other, his footsteps echoing hollowly. The typewriters slept beneath their covers. The big cupboard doors had closed on their shelves of well ordered files. Ten years of work and experience. He felt as though he were visiting the vaults of a bank – there where there lies a weight of gold. But each of these registers had accumulated a finer stuff than gold – a stock of living energy. Living but asleep, like hoarded gold.

Somewhere he would come upon the only clerk on night duty. The man was working somewhere so that the life of the company should know no break, so that everything might be infused with a steady determination, so that, from Toulouse to Buenos Aires, each airfield should be part of the same unbroken chain.

'That fellow,' thought Rivière, 'doesn't realize his greatness.' Somewhere in these southern skies the mail-planes were battling their way forward. A night flight was like an illness over which one had to keep watch. One had to help these men who, with their hands and knees, chest against chest, were wrestling with the dark, who were locked in a struggle with unseen, shifting things, from whose fateful grip their blind arms had to pull them, as from a sea. What dreadful admissions he had sometimes heard! 'I lit the lamp to see my hands ...' The velvet texture of a pair of hands revealed in this dark-room glow – all that was left of the world and which must be saved.

Rivière pushed open the door of the Traffic Office. A solitary lamp in one corner made a luminous beach. The clicking of a single typewriter gave meaning to the silence, without filling it. Now and then the telephone buzzer sounded; whereupon the duty clerk got up and walked towards this sad, obstinate, repeated call. The duty clerk lifted the receiver and the invisible anguish was soothed by a soft exchange of murmurs in a shadowy corner. Then the man returned to his office, his solitude- and sleep-drawn features closed over some hermetic secret. What a latent menace there is in a call coming from the outer night when two mail-planes are in the air! Rivière thought of the telegrams which reach families under the evening lamp-light, then of the grief which for several seemingly eternal seconds remains a secret on the father's face. At first no more than a ripple, so soft, so remote from the distantly uttered cry. It was its faint echo he caught each time the telephone sounded its discreet buzzer. And each time he saw the clerk emerging from the shadows towards the lamp-light, like a diver ascending from the depths, his slow, solitary, deliberate movements struck him as heavy with secrets.

'Don't move. I'll take it.'

Rivière lifted the receiver and heard the buzzing of the outer world.

'Rivière speaking.'

There was a confused sound, then a voice: 'I'm connecting you to the radio station.'

There was a new crackling, as the operator plugged into the switchboard, then another voice came through: 'This is the radio centre. Here are the latest telegrams.'

Rivière took them down, nodding his head as he did so:

'Good . . . Good . . .'

Nothing of importance. The usual service messages. Rio de Janeiro asking for information, Montevideo reporting on the weather, Mendoza on a question of equipment. Familiar household noises.

'And the mail-planes?'

'There's thunder in the air. We can't hear them.'

'I see.'

The night was fine and starry, Rivière reflected, yet in it the radio operators could detect the breath of distant storms.

'Ring me back.'

As Rivière rose, the clerk came up to him. 'Some papers to be signed, sir.'

'All right.'

Rivière felt a mounting fondness for this man, upon whom the night also weighed. 'A comrade-in-arms,' he thought. 'And who may never know how much this vigil has brought us together.'

9

As he was walking back to his office with a sheaf of papers in his hand, Rivière felt a stab of pain in his right side. For some weeks now it had been bothering him.

'Bad . . .'

He leaned for a moment against the wall.

'How ridiculous!' he thought, as he made his way to his chair.

Once again he felt himself chained up, like an ageing lion, and a great sadness came over him.

'So much work and effort to end up like this! I'm fifty years old. At fifty I've had a full life, I've struggled, I've altered the course of events, yet here I am tormented by something that makes everything else seem trifling . . . Ridiculous!'

He paused, wiped away several drops of sweat, and when the pain had eased, he set to work on the memoranda.

'In taking down Motor 301 in Buenos Aires we discovered that . . . The person responsible will be severely fined.'

He signed.

'The Florianopolis airfield, having failed to heed instructions . . .'

He signed.

'As a disciplinary measure we are transferring airfield controller Richard for having . . .'

He signed.

Slumbering but ever present in him, like a new meaning of life, the pain in his side brought his thoughts back on himself.

'Am I being fair or not?' he wondered, almost bitterly. 'I

don't know. If I bear down hard, the accidents diminish. It isn't the individual who's responsible; it's an obscure power that can only be dealt with if everyone is affected. If I were really fair and just, each night flight would involve a risk of death.'

He felt a certain weariness at having traced so hard a road. Pity, he thought, is good. He leafed through the papers, absorbed in his reflections.

'... As for Roblet, as of today he is no longer part of our personnel.'

He recalled the talk he had had with the old fellow the evening before.

'An example, you understand, is an example.'

'But Monsieur ... but Monsieur ... It was only once, one single time, just think! I who've worked all my life!'

'An example must be made.'

'But Monsieur! ... Look, Monsieur!'

He had produced a tattered pocket-book and pulled from it a yellowed newspaper page which showed Roblet posing in front of a plane. Rivière had seen the old hands trembling over this naive glory.

'This dates from 1910, Monsieur ... It was me here assembled the first plane in Argentina! I've been in aviation since 1910, Monsieur ... Twenty years, that makes! So how can you say ... And the young 'uns, Monsieur, how they'll be laughing in the workshops! ... Oh, but how they'll laugh!'

'I can't help that.'

'And my kids, Monsieur, my kids!'

'I told you – you can stay on as an odd job man.'

'But my dignity, Monsieur, my dignity! Just think, Monsieur, twenty years of aviation, an old worker like me ...'

'As an odd job man, I said.'

'I refuse, Monsieur, I refuse!'

The old hands had trembled, and Rivière had had to avert his eyes from that thick, wrinkled, lovely skin.

'As an odd job man . . .'

'No, Monsieur, no . . . And there's something else I want to say –'

'That will do.'

'It wasn't him I was so brutally dismissing,' thought Rivière, 'it was the trouble for which he's perhaps not responsible but of which he's the agent. Men are paltry things, and they too must be created. Or eliminated when they bring bad luck.'

'And there's something else I want to say . . .' What had the poor fellow meant by that? That he was being deprived of his old joys? That he enjoyed the sound of his tools against the steel of the planes, that his life would be robbed of its poetry . . . and then, a man must live?

'I'm tired,' thought Rivière, feeling faintly feverish. He drummed his finger on the sheet of paper. 'I liked that old worker's face . . .' Rivière thought of his hands, of the tiny movement that could have brought them together. He had only needed to say: 'All right. All right. You can stay.' Rivière imagined the joy which would have gushed through those old hands. And the joy which those old workman's hands, even more than his face, would have expressed struck him as the loveliest thing in all the world. 'Shall I tear up this memorandum?'

And what a homecoming in the evening, what a modest pride in the presence of the family!

'So they're keeping you on?'

'What do you think! It was me assembled the first plane in Argentina!'

And the young ones who would no longer laugh at the old timer's lost prestige . . .

'Shall I tear it up?'

The telephone rang. Rivière lifted the receiver. There was a long pause, then that resonance, that depth which the wind and space lend to human voices. Finally a voice spoke:

'Airfield here. Who's that?'

'Rivière.'

'Monsieur le Directeur, the 650 is on the field and ready.'

'Good.'

'Well, everything's now under control. But at the last moment we had to redo the electric circuit, there were some faulty connections.'

'I see. Who did the wiring?'

'We'll check. And with your permission we'll take the necessary disciplinary action. A light failure on the instrument panel can be a serious matter.'

'Of course.'

'If,' Rivière thought, 'one doesn't uproot the trouble wherever one meets it, light failures will occur. It would have been criminal to have found it out only when the pilot had to light up his instruments. Roblet shall go.'

The clerk, who had seen nothing, was still typing away.

'What's that?'

'The fortnightly accounts.'

'Why aren't they ready?'

'I . . .'

'I'll look into it.'

Strange, how easily events get the upper hand! Rivière thought of those clinging vines that are strong enough to bring down temples. It was the same elemental force at work in the rain forests, the same upheaving force which threatens any great undertaking.

'A great undertaking . . .'

To reassure himself added: 'I like all of these men. It's not them I'm fighting, it's the ill that passes through them.'

He could feel his heart beat faster and it hurt him.

'I don't know if what I've done is good. I don't know the exact value of human life, nor of justice, nor of grief. I don't know exactly what a man's joy is worth. Nor a trembling hand. Nor pity, nor kindness . . .

'Life is so full of contradictions,' he reflected. 'One manages as best one can . . . But creating, making things last, exchanging one's perishable body . . .?'

Rivière, after a moment of reflection, rang his bell.

'Telephone the pilot of the Europe-bound plane and tell him to come and see me before taking off.'

'There's no point,' he thought, 'in the mail-plane's pointlessly turning back. If I don't shake my men up, the night will always unnerve them.'

10

Woken by the telephone, the pilot's wife looked at her husband and thought: 'I'll let him sleep a little longer.'

She gazed admiringly at his naked chest, beautifully rounded like a ship's hull. He lay in this calm bed, as in a harbour, and lest anything disturb his slumbers, she smoothed out this fold, this shadow, this wave, with her finger, stilling this bed as a divine finger does the sea.

She got up and opened the window. The wind hit her in the face. Their bedroom overlooked Buenos Aires. People were dancing in a near-by house, the wind brought the sound of music, for it was the hour of pleasure and repose. The city had packed its inhabitants into a hundred thousand fortresses: everything was peaceful and secure; but it seemed to this woman that a cry would soon ring out: 'To arms!' and that only one man, her own, would rise up in answer. He was still resting, but his rest was the redoubtable, fragile repose of reserves soon to be committed. This sleeping city offered him no protection: vain would soon seem its lights when, like a young god, he soared above their glittering dust. She looked at those stout arms which in an hour's time would shoulder the burden of the Europe-bound mail and be responsible for something big, like the fate of a city.

The thought troubled her. That this man, among millions of others, was alone prepared for this strange sacrifice made her sad. He would soon be beyond the range of her tenderness. She had fed him, watched over him, caressed him not for herself but for this night which was going to claim him. For struggles, anxieties, and victories she would never know anything about. Those tender hands of his had merely been tamed, and the real work for which they were destined remained obscure. She knew this man's smiles, his thoughtfulness as a lover, but not his godlike fury in a storm. She burdened him with tender links – music, love, flowers – but at the moment of each take-off these links were cast off without his seeming to feel regret.

He opened his eyes.

'What's the time?'

'Midnight.'

'How's the weather?'

'I don't know.'

He got up, and stretching lazily, walked towards the window.

'I shouldn't be too cold. Which way is the wind blowing?'

'How should I know?'

He leaned out. 'From the south. That's fine. It should hold as far as Brazil.'

He looked up at the moon and felt like a millionaire. Then he looked down on the city, finding it neither kind nor luminous nor warm. He could already see its lights . . . draining out their vain sands.

'What are you thinking of?'

He was thinking of the fog he might run into in the region of Porto Allegre.

'I've worked out my tactics. I know exactly how to get around it.'

He was still bent over the window-sill, inhaling deeply, as though about to dive naked into the sea.

'You're not even sad . . . How many days will you be gone?'

Eight, ten days, he didn't know. Sad, no . . . why? Those plains, those towns, those mountains . . . He was setting forth like a free man on their conquest. In an hour's time Buenos Aires would have been vanquished and then discarded behind him.

He smiled: 'This city . . . I'll soon be far from it. It's a lovely thing, leaving at night. You pull the throttle lever all the way back, head south, and ten seconds later you swing the landscape round and head north. The city disappears, like an ocean bottom.'

She thought of all the things a man must reject in order to conquer.

'Don't you like your home?'

'I do like my home.'

But his wife knew that he was already on his way. His broad shoulders were already bearing into the sky.

She pointed to it. 'You've got lovely weather, your route is paved with stars.'

'Yes,' he laughed.

She laid her hand on his shoulder: it seemed almost unnaturally warm, as though the flesh were threatened by some inner ferment.

'You're very strong, I know, but do be careful!'

'Careful? Of course . . .' And he laughed again.

He began dressing. For this fiesta he chose the roughest materials, the heaviest of leather gear, he dressed like a peasant. The heavier he grew, the more she admired him. She buckled his belt herself, helped him pull on his boots.

'These boots are too tight.'

'Here are the others.'

'Fetch me a piece of cord for the emergency lamp.'

She looked at him. She was helping to repair the last chinks in the armour. Now everything was set.

'You look wonderful.'

She watched him, carefully combing his hair.

'Is it for the stars?'

'So I won't start feeling old . . .'

'I'm jealous . . .'

He laughed again and kissed her, pressing her against his heavy togs. Then he lifted her up on outstretched arms, much as one lifts a little girl, and still laughing, he laid her out on the bed.

'Now go to sleep!'

Closing the door behind him, he descended into the street. Here, in the midst of the anonymous night crowd, he took his first conquering steps.

She remained behind, gazing sadly at the flowers, the books, the tender souvenirs – for him a mere ocean bottom.

II

Rivière greeted him: 'That was a neat one you pulled on me during your last flight. Turning back when the weather reports were good. You could have pushed through. You were scared?'

Taken aback, the pilot said nothing. He rubbed his hands slowly against each other. Then he raised his head and looked Rivière in the eyes.

'Yes.'

Rivière felt sorry for this brave fellow who had taken fright. The pilot sought to apologize.

'I couldn't see a blessed thing. I know . . . further on perhaps . . . The radio said so . . . But my panel lamp got so dim I couldn't even see my hands. I tried switching on my wing-light, but I couldn't see that either. It was like being at the bottom of a deep hole it's hard to climb out of. And then, my engine began vibrating . . .'

'No.'

'No?'

'No. We had a look at it afterwards. It was in perfect shape. But one always thinks an engine's vibrating when one's scared.'

'Who wouldn't have been scared! There were mountains all round and above me. When I tried climbing, I ran into a lot of turbulence. You know – when one's as blind as a bat – the downdraughts . . . Instead of climbing, I lost three hundred feet. I couldn't see the artificial horizon, I couldn't even see the oil-pressure gauge any more. I had the impression my engine was losing speed, that it was heating up and the oil pressure going down . . . And all of it in the dark, like a tomb. I was damned glad to see the lights of the first town again.'

'You've got too much imagination. Now be off with you.'

And the pilot left him.

*

Rivière sank back in his chair and ran his fingers through his grey hair.

'He's the bravest of my men,' he thought. 'That was a fine piece of piloting the other night, but even so . . . I rescue him from fear.'

For a moment he yielded to a new wave of indulgence. 'To make oneself loved, it's enough to show pity. I show scant pity, or I hide it. Yet I wouldn't mind surrounding myself with friendship and human kindness. A doctor encounters them in his profession. But I'm the servant of events. I must forge men so that they can serve them too. How harshly I feel this iron law, here in my office in the evening when I'm alone with the flight reports. But if I let myself go, if I let events take their well ordered course, then accidents mysteriously occur. As though it were my sole will which kept the plane from cracking up in flight, or the storm from slowing down the mail. Sometimes I'm surprised by my own power.

'Probably it's quite straightforward,' he mused on. 'Like the gardener's never-ending struggle with his lawn. It's the simple weight of his hand, bearing down ceaselessly upon it, which keeps the earth from throwing up a jungle.'

He thought of the pilot. 'I'm rescuing him from fear. It's not him I was attacking, but through him that resistance which paralyses men in the face of the unknown. If I listen to him, if I feel sorry for him, if I take his apprehensions seriously, he will think he's returning from a land of mystery, and mystery alone is what one is afraid of. There must be no more mystery. The men must descend into this dark well, and then come up again saying they've found nothing. This man must descend into the innermost heart of the night, in all its depth, and without so much as that little miner's lamp which, though it only lights up the hands or the wing, keeps the unknown at arm's length.'

*

Yet in this battle a silent fraternity bound Rivière to his pilots. They were crew mates, fired with the same desire to vanquish. But Rivière recalled the other battles he had had to wage for the conquest of the night. In official circles this dark territory was feared like an unexplored hinterland. The idea of launching a crew at 140 miles an hour against the thunderstorms and mists and all the material obstacles that night secretes, seemed to them an adventure which was tolerable for military aviation: when the night is clear one takes off, drops bombs, and returns to the same field. But regular mail flights were bound to fail. 'For us,' Rivière had replied, 'it's a matter of life and death, since we lose at night the lead we gain each day on the railways and steamships.'

Rivière had been forced to listen to much boring talk about balance-sheets, insurance rates, and, above all, public opinion. 'Public opinion,' he retorted, 'is something one guides, one governs.' What a waste of time! he had thought. 'There's something . . . something infinitely more important than all this. A thing which is really alive upsets everything, it generates its own laws for living. It's irresistible.' Rivière had no idea when or how commercial aviation would undertake night flights, but one had to prepare for this unavoidable solution.

He recalled those green baize table covers in front of which, his chin resting on his fist, he had had to listen to so many objections. How vain they had seemed to him, how condemned in advance by life! And with them he had felt his own strength gathering weight within him. 'My reasons carry weight, I'll win,' Rivière had thought. 'It's the natural slope of events.' When they asked him for perfect solutions, guaranteed to eliminate all risks, he would reply: 'Experience will establish the necessary laws. The proper understanding of laws never precedes experience.'

Rivière had finally won, after a long year of battling. For some it was 'because of his faith', for others 'because of his bear-like tenacity and toughness'. But for him it was simply because he was leaning in the right direction.

But how cautious the first steps had been! The planes only took off one hour before sunrise and landed one hour after sunset. Only when Rivière felt surer of his ground did he dare push his mail-planes into the depth of the night. Backed up by almost nobody, disowned by nearly all, he now waged a lonely battle.

Rivière rang, to get the latest messages from the planes in flight.

12

The Patagonia mail-plane was now entering the storm. Fabien gave up all thought of trying to fly around it: its front was too broad, and the battle-line of lightning flashes extended far inland, revealing mighty fortresses of cloud. He would try to slip through underneath, and if the going got too rough, he would turn and fly out.

He glanced at his altimeter: 1,700 metres. He pressed the palms of his hands against the controls to lose height. The engine throbbed wildly and the plane began to tremble. Fabien corrected the angle of descent, then looked at the map to check the height of the hills beneath him. 500 metres. To keep a safe margin he would fly at 700. He was sacrificing his altitude as one stakes a fortune.

The plane lurched, trembling, into an air pocket. Fabien felt himself threatened by invisible landslides. He thought wistfully of turning back to find his hundred thousand stars, but he did not shift his course by one degree.

Fabien calculated his chances. Probably this was a local storm; for Trelew, the next port-of-call, reported a sky that was only three-quarters overcast. He had just twenty more minutes of this inky concrete to endure. Yet the pilot felt uneasy. Hunched over to the left, into the teeth of the wind, he sought to interpret those confused glows which permeate even the most opaque of nights. But there was now not even a glow: only changes of density in the surrounding darkness, or was it a fatigue of the eyes?

He unfolded a slip of paper handed to him by the radio operator: 'Where are we?'

Fabien would have given a great deal to know. He scribbled back: 'Don't know. We're crossing storm by compass.'

He hunched over once again. He was bothered by the exhaust flame ahead of him, pinned to the engine like a bouquet of fire, so pale that the moonlight would have extinguished it, but which in this inky void absorbed the visible world. He watched it – braided stiffly by the wind, like a torch flame.

Every thirty seconds, to check his gyroscope and compass readings, Fabien ducked his head down inside the cockpit. He no longer dared light the dim red panel-lamps which would have blinded him for too long an interval, but the dials with their radium-tinted numbers emitted a pale star-like glow. Here, amid dial-hands and figures, the pilot experienced a deceptive security, such as one feels in a ship's cabin overswept by waves. The night, and all it secreted of rocks and reefs and wreckage, came billowing up against the plane with the same startling fatality.

'Where are we?' again queried the radio operator.

Fabien had straightened up and resumed his grim watch, bent over to the left for a better view beyond the motor. He had no idea how much time or effort it would take to deliver himself from these dark thongs, or if he would ever be freed of them. He was gambling his life on the brief message scrawled on this dirty, crumpled slip of paper he had unfolded and re-read a thousand times, to sustain his hopes: 'Trelew: sky three-quarters overcast, weak west wind.' If Trelew was three-quarters overcast, its lights could soon be spotted through a rift in the clouds. Unless . . .

The pale glow promised him up ahead prompted him to carry on. But to still his doubts he scribbled back to the radio operator: 'Don't know if I can get through. Find out if weather's still fine behind.'

The reply appalled him:

'Comodoro reports: return here impossible. Storm.'

He was beginning to take the measure of this unusual offensive, launched from the cordillera of the Andes towards the sea. Before he could reach them, the cyclone would have scooped up all the towns.

'Ask state of weather at San Antonio.'

'Reply from Antonio: rising west wind, storm to west. Sky four-quarters overcast. San Antonio receiving very badly because of static. I'm hearing badly too. May have to haul in aerial soon because of lightning discharges. Are you turning back? What are your plans?'

'Stuff your questions. Ask for weather at Bahía Blanca.'

'Reply from Bahía Blanca : violent west gale expected over Bahía Blanca in next twenty minutes.'

'Ask for weather at Trelew.'

'Reply from Trelew : west gale force thirty metres per second and rain squalls.'

'Radio to Buenos Aires : blocked on all sides, storm developing thousand kilometre front, visibility nil. What should we do?'

*

This night for the pilot was without a landfall. It led to no port (for they all seemed inaccessible), still less towards the sun. In an hour and forty minutes the fuel supply would be exhausted. Sooner or later they would be forced to founder blindly in this sea of pitch.

If only he could make it through to dawn! Fabien thought of the dawn as of a golden strand on to which they would have been cast up after this rough night. Beneath the threatened craft the plains would spread their crib. The tranquil earth would heave into view, carrying its sleeping farms and the flocks upon its hills. Night dispelled, the storm-tossed derelicts would no longer threaten rack and ruin. If he could have done so, how he would have swum towards the daylight!

But now he was encircled. Everything, for good or ill, would be resolved in this thick murk. Yes, it was true: the onset of day was like a convalescence. He had felt it more than once, but never more poignantly than now. What good was it to train one's eyes on the east, the sun's distant home? Between them now there lay such an abyss of night that from its depths never could he rise.

13

'The Asunción mail-plane is doing well. It should get in around two o'clock. On the other hand, the Patagonia mail-plane seems to be in trouble and we can anticipate a serious delay.'

'Yes, Monsieur Rivière.'

'We may possibly not wait for its arrival before having the Europe plane take off. As soon as Asunción is in, you'll ring me for instructions. Meanwhile stand by.'

Rivière now scanned the weather reports from the airfields to the north. They promised the Europe-bound mail-plane a perfect moonlit ride. 'Sky clear, full moon, no wind.' The mountains of Brazil, darkly silhouetted against the moon-flooded heavens, plunged their shocks of jet-black forest into the silvery undulations of the sea. Those forests upon which, without colouring them, the moonbeams unwearingly rained down. Black too were the islands, floating on the sea like derelicts. And above them all the moon, that fount of light!

If Rivière ordered the take-off, the crew of the Europe-bound mail-plane would enter a stable world, softly glowing all night long. A world in which nothing threatened the equilibrium of shadowed masses and wells of light. A world unruffled by the faintest caress of those pure winds which, though they cool, can spoil an entire sky in a couple of hours.

Yet Rivière hesitated before this beckoning radiance, like a prospector in front of forbidden goldfields. The situation in the south threatened to prove him wrong. From a disaster in Patagonia his adversaries could derive such moral backing that it might well reduce his faith to impotence. Rivière was the sole champion of night flights, but his faith remained unshaken. A flaw in his work had made the crisis possible: the crisis had shown up the flaw, it proved nothing more. 'We may need observation posts in the west. It's something we'll look into,' he thought. 'I'll have the same solid reasons for insisting. It will be one less possible cause of accident, the one that's now shown up.'

Strong men are fortified by setbacks. Unfortunately, in dealing with men one plays a game in which the real meaning of things counts for little. People win or lose on the basis of appearances, and the points gained are trivial. A semblance of defeat is enough to hamstring one completely.

Rivière rang his bell.

'Still no messages from Bahía Blanca?'

'No.'

'Get me the airfield by telephone.'

Five minutes later he was through.

'Why haven't you been radioing anything?'

'We can't hear the mail-plane.'

'Is he silent?'

'We don't know. There's too much thunder. Even if he was tapping something out, we'd hear nothing.'

'Can Trelew hear him?'

'We can't hear Trelew.'

'Then telephone.'

'We've tried, but the line's cut.'

'What's your weather like?'

'Pretty threatening. Lightning to west and south. Very sultry.'

'Any wind?'

'Still weak, but probably not for more than ten minutes. The lightning flashes are moving up fast.'

There was a pause.

'Bahía Blanca? Are you listening? Good. Call back in ten minutes.'

Rivière leafed through the telegrams from the southern airfields. All alike reported: no message from the plane. Some stations no longer answered Buenos Aires. The patch of silence was spreading across the map, as the little towns were swallowed up by the cyclone, their bolted doors and lightless streets as cut off from the world and lost in the night as a ship. Dawn alone would deliver them.

Bent over the map, Rivière still hoped against hope to discover a tiny haven of clear sky. He had dispatched telegrams to thirty provincial police-stations requesting information on the weather. The replies were beginning to come in. Over a distance of twelve hundred miles the radio stations were instructed to notify Buenos Aires within thirty seconds if one of them intercepted an appeal from the plane, so that the position of the haven could be relayed back to Fabien.

The secretaries, reporting for night duty at 1 a.m., were now in their offices. Hurried whispers made it known that night flights would probably be suspended, and that the Europe-bound mail would not take off before dawn. They spoke in hushed tones of Fabien, the cyclone, and above all of Rivière, whom they could picture near by, crushed by the growing magnitude of this elemental rebuff.

Abruptly the chattering stopped. Rivière had just appeared, pausing by his door in his overcoat, the hat still pulled down over the eyes, like the eternal voyager he seemed to be. He stepped quietly up to the head clerk.

'It's 1.10. Are the clearance papers for the Europe mail in order?'

'I . . . I thought –'

'You're not here to think, but to carry out orders.'

He turned slowly on his heel and walked over to an open window, his hands clasped behind his back.

A secretary caught up with him: 'Monsieur le Directeur, we won't be getting many replies. We've been informed that inland many telephone lines are already down.'

'I see.'

Without moving a muscle Rivière stared out at the night.

*

Thus each new message boded new peril for the mail. Each town able to reply before the telephone lines were wrecked reported the advance of the cyclone, like that of an invasion. 'It's coming from the interior, from the cordillera. It's sweeping everything before it towards the sea . . .'

Rivière looked up at the stars. They were too bright and the air was too humid. What a strange night! It was rotting away in patches, like the flesh of a glowing peach. The stars in all their glory still shone down on Buenos Aires, but they were no more than an oasis, and a temporary one at that. A haven which in any case was beyond Fabien's reach. A night of menace, touched and tainted by an evil wind. A difficult night to overcome.

Somewhere in its depths a plane was in peril; but here on the bank one waved one's arms in vain.

14

Fabien's wife telephoned.

Each time he was due back she would calculate the progress of the Patagonia mail-plane. 'He's now taking off from Trelew . . .' And she would go back to sleep. A little later: 'He must be approaching San Antonio, he should be able to see its lights . . .' She would then get up, throw back the curtains, and question the sky. 'Those clouds will bother him . . .' At times the moon was there, ready to shepherd him across the heavens. Whereupon the young wife went back to bed, reassured by the moon and the stars, by those thousand and one presences hovering over her husband. Towards one o'clock she would feel him drawing near. 'He can't be far off now, he must be in sight of Buenos Aires . . .' She then got up once more and prepared a meal for him, with a pot of hot coffee. 'It's so cold up there . . .' She always welcomed him back as though he had just descended from some snowy summit. 'Aren't you cold?' 'Why no.' 'Well, warm yourself anyway . . .' At 1.15, when everything was ready, she would telephone.

Tonight, as on the others, she rang up to get the news.

'Has Fabien landed?'

The secretary at the other end began to fumble for his words.

'Who's speaking?'

'Simone Fabien.'

'Ah ! Just a moment . . .'

Not daring to say anything, the secretary passed the receiver to the head clerk.

'Who is it?'

'Simone Fabien.'

'Ah ! . . . What can I do for you, Madame?'

'Has my husband landed?'

There was a baffling silence, followed by this simple reply: 'No.'

'Has he been held up?'

'Yes.'

There was another silence. 'Yes, he's been held up.'

'Ah !'

That 'Ah !' was the cry of a wounded creature. Being held up is nothing . . . is nothing . . . but when it lasts too long . . .

'Ah ! . . . And when is he expected in?'

'When's he expected in? We . . . we don't know exactly.'

It was like talking to a wall. All she was getting now was echoes of her own questions.

'Do please tell me, give me an answer ! Where is he?'

'Where is he? Wait . . .'

The suspense was painful. Something was going on there, behind that wall.

An answer was finally forthcoming.

'He took off from Comodoro at 19.30.'

'And since then?'

'Since then? . . . He's been seriously delayed . . . seriously delayed by bad weather . . .'

'Ah ! Bad weather !'

What injustice, what sly deceit on the part of that lazy moon, languidly stretched out up there over Buenos Aires ! Suddenly the young wife remembered that barely two hours were needed to fly from Comodoro to Trelew.

'And he's been flying six hours towards Trelew ! But he's been sending out messages ! What's he been saying?'

'What's he been saying? Naturally . . . with this kind of weather . . . you understand . . . his messages haven't been getting through . . .'

'This kind of weather !'

'Madame, rest assured. We'll call you the moment we know something.'

'Oh ! So you know nothing !'

'Good-bye, Madame . . .'

'No ! No ! I want to talk to the Director.'

'Monsieur le Directeur is very busy, Madame, he's got someone in his office . . .'

'Well, I don't care ! I don't care ! I want to talk to him !'

The head clerk mopped his brow. 'Just a moment, please . . .'

He pushed open Rivière's door.

'It's Madame Fabien . . . wants to speak to you . . .'

'What I was dreading !' thought Rivière. The emotional facets of the crisis were beginning to manifest themselves. His first impulse was to brush them aside: mothers and wives are not admitted to Operations Rooms. Emotional outbursts are likewise silenced on a ship in danger. They are no help in saving lives. Nevertheless he agreed to take the call.

'Switch it through to my office.'

He heard that distant, trembling voice and instantly realized that he could give her no answer. It would be pointless, utterly futile for them to meet face to face.

'Madame, I beg you, please calm yourself! In our profession we often have to wait a long time for news.'

He had reached that frontier where the issue was not a tiny individual distress, but the problem posed by action. Facing Rivière now was not Fabien's wife, but another form of life. Rivière could only listen, could only pity that small voice, that desperate plaint, but it was that of the enemy. For action and individual happiness know no quarter : they are in conflict. This woman also was speaking in the name of a world of absolute rights and duties – that of the lamp-light on the evening table, of a flesh which claims its flesh, of a homeland of hopes, affections, and remembrances. She claimed her own and she was right. Rivière too was right; but he could oppose nothing to this woman's truth. His own truth was revealed to him in the light of a humble domestic lamp – inexpressible, inhuman . . .

'Madame . . .'

She was no longer listening. She had slumped down, it seemed to him, at his feet, her feeble fists exhausted from beating on the wall.

*

An engineer had one day said to Rivière, as they were bending over an injured man, near a bridge that was being built : 'Is this bridge worth the price of a crushed face?' Not one of the peasants for whom this road was being opened would have agreed in advance to the mutilation of this face, simply to spare himself a detour via the next bridge. Yet one went on building bridges. The engineer had added : 'The general interest is made up of individual interests : it does not justify anything else.'

'And yet,' Rivière had replied to him later, 'if human life is priceless, we always act as though there was something exceeding human life in value . . . But what?'

Now, thinking of the airborne crew, Rivière felt a pang. Action, even that involved in the building of a bridge, breaks hearts, and Rivière could no longer avoid asking himself 'in the name of what?'

'These men,' he thought, 'who are perhaps doomed to disappear, could have lived happily.' He imagined their faces crowded around the golden sanctuary of evening lamps. 'In the name of what did I tear them from it?' In the name of what had he torn them from individual happiness? Was not one's first obligation to protect this kind of happiness? Yet he himself was shattering it. Still, the golden sanctuaries one day vanish inexorably like mirages. Old age and death destroy them, even more pitilessly than he. Perhaps there is something else, something more enduring to be saved; and perhaps it was to save this part of man that Rivière was working? Otherwise, the action would have no justification.

*

'To love, only to love, what an impasse!' Rivière had the obscure sentiment of a duty greater than that of loving. Or perhaps it was also a form of affection, but so different from the rest. A phrase came back to him: 'It's a question of making them eternal ...' Where had he read that? 'That which you seek within yourself will die.' He recalled a temple erected by the ancient Incas of Peru in honour of the Sun-God, those sharp-cut stones against the mountainside. But for them what would there be left of a powerful civilization which now weighed, with all the weight of its massive stones, like a reproach on contemporary man? 'In the name of what harshness, of what strange love did the leader of men of yore force the multitudes to drag this temple up the mountain, thus compelling them to erect their own eternity?' And there arose in Rivière's mind the vision of the crowds in little provincial towns, strolling around their bandstands in the evening. 'This kind of happiness, this harness ...' he thought. But the leader of men of yore, if he felt scant pity for man's sufferings, felt a boundless pity for his death. Not for his individual death, but pity for the species, doomed one day to be erased like footprints in the sand. And he drove his people to erect stones which the desert would not bury.

15

This slip of neatly folded paper might perhaps save him: Fabien unfolded it, his jaw grimly set.

'Can't get through to Buenos Aires. Can't even tap out a message, getting electric shocks in my fingers.'

Irritated, Fabien wanted to reply, but the moment he took his hands off the controls to write, he felt his body heaved up by a mighty groundswell. The air currents lifted him up, along with his five tons of metal, and tossed him about. He abandoned the attempt. His hands closed back on the wave and steadied its wild surge.

Fabien took a deep breath. If the radio operator hauled up the aerial because he was afraid of the lightning, he would punch his face in when they landed. They absolutely had to get in touch with Buenos Aires – as though from a distance of a thousand miles a life-line could be thrown to them in this abyss. In the absence of a trembling light, of an inn-lamp's distant glimmer – useless, to be sure, but which, like a beacon, would have proved the proximity of solid land – he needed a voice, just one, come from a world which had ceased to exist. The pilot raised and shook his fist in the reddish glow, to make the man behind understand this tragic truth, but the latter failed to see it, fixed as his eyes were on the wasteland below, with its dead lights and buried towns.

Fabien would have heeded any advice if only it could have been shouted through to him. 'If they tell me to fly round in circles, I'll fly round in circles, and if they tell me to fly due south . . .' Somewhere they still existed, those lands of calm, moon-shadowed peace. Down there, like learned scientists, his omniscient companions were bent over their maps, sheltered by lamps as soft as flowers. But all it was given him to know was the turbulence of this black night, which kept pounding him with landslides and cataracts. How could they abandon these two men amid these downpours and flame-filled clouds? How could they? 'Set course at 240 degrees . . .' they would order Fabien, and he would shift his course to 240. But he was alone.

Even the brute matter, it now seemed to him, began to mutiny. With each new plunge the engine began vibrating so violently that the entire plane was seized with angry trembling. Fabien needed all his strength to control it. His head ducked far down inside the cockpit, he kept his eyes glued to the artificial horizon; for outside he could no longer distinguish earth from sky, lost in a welter of primeval darkness. But now the instrument needles in front of him began oscillating wildly, growing increasingly difficult to follow. Misled by their erratic readings, he lost altitude. Slowly but surely he was sinking into a dark morass, a murky quicksand. The heading on his altimeter was now '500 metres' – the height of the hilltops beneath him. He could feel them heaving up their towering breakers towards him. It was as though all these land masses, the tiniest of which could have smashed him to smithereens, had suddenly been ripped from their foundations and unhinged and were now beginning to career drunkenly around him. A deadly dance had begun, tightening about him like a noose.

He made up his mind. He could land no matter where, even at the risk of cracking up. But to avoid the hills, at least, he threw out his one and only flare. It burst briefly into flame, as it spun downward, cast its eerie glow over a plain, then died: it was the sea.

The thoughts raced through his mind. 'I'm lost. Even with a 40 degree wind correction, I've drifted off course. It's a gale. Where's the land?'

He banked, heading now due west. 'Without a flare to guide me I'm a goner,' he thought. 'Well, it was bound to happen one day.' As for the fellow behind him . . . 'He's certain to have pulled in the aerial.' But he was no longer angry with him. He had only to let go with both hands and their lives would be scattered like dust. In his hands he held the beating heart of his companion and his own. Now suddenly his hands appalled him.

At each new hammer-blow he had gripped the stick with redoubled strength, to temper the jerks which otherwise would have snapped the cables. He still hung on grimly. But now he could no longer feel his hands, numbed by the effort. He tried to move his fingers, to receive some impulse from them, but he could not tell if he was being obeyed. His arms ended in strange, almost foreign appendages – flabby and unfeeling flaps. 'I must concentrate on thinking – I'm gripping.' He could not tell if his thought reached his hands; for it was through the pain in his shoulders that he felt the buffets to the stick. 'It's going to get away from me,' he thought. 'My hands are going to open . . .' The mere idea that he could entertain such a thought frightened him; for he now had the impression that his hands were slowly opening in the dark and releasing their vital grip in response to the sombre image of his imagination.

He might have kept up the struggle for some time and tried his luck. There is no such thing as external fate; its real working is internal. There comes a moment when one realizes how vulnerable one is, and then the blunders suck you down, like a whirlpool.

At this very moment the storm opened above his head and through a rift, like mortal bait glittering through the meshes of a net, he spied several stars. He sensed it was a trap: one sees three stars in a hole, one rises towards them, and then one can no longer come down, one stays up there to nibble at the stars . . .

But such was his thirst for light that he began to climb.

16

As he climbed, he found it easier to counteract the air currents by taking his bearings on the stars. Their pale magnets attracted him. He had struggled so long for a glimpse of light that now he would not have let even the faintest get away from him. Having found the inn-lamp he yearned for, he would have circled round this coveted sign till death. And thus he rose towards these fields of light.

Little by little he spiralled up in the well that had opened and which closed again beneath him. As he rose the clouds lost their muddy shadows, they swept against him in ever purer, ever whiter waves. Fabien rose clear.

His surprise was extreme. The brightness was such that it dazzled him, and for several seconds he had to close his eyes. He never would have thought that the clouds at night could dazzle. But the full moon and the constellations had changed them into radiant billows.

At a single bound, as it emerged, the plane had attained a calm that seemed wondrous. There was not a wave to rock him, and like a sail-boat passing the jetty he was entering sheltered waters. He had found refuge in some uncharted spot of sky, as hidden as the bay of the Happy Isles. Beneath him, nine thousand feet deep, the storm formed another world, shot through with gusts and cloudbursts and lightning flashes, but towards the stars it turned a surface of snowy crystal.

Fabien felt as though he had reached some strange limbo, for everything now grew luminous – his hands, his flying togs, his wings. For the light did not stream down from the stars: rather it welled up from underneath and around him from these endless white drifts. The clouds beneath him reflected back the snow shed on them by the moon, as did those banked up to right and left of him like towers. The two of them were floating through a milky stream of light. Fabien, when he looked round, saw the radio operator smiling.

'We're doing better!' he cried.

But the sound was lost in the roar of the flight, and the smiles alone came through. 'I must be mad to smile,' thought Fabien. 'We're lost!'

A thousand dark arms had relinquished their grip on him. His bonds had been loosened, like those of a prisoner allowed to walk for a while alone among the flowers.

'Too beautiful,' thought Fabien. He was wandering through a dense treasure-hoard of stars, in a world where nothing, absolutely nothing else but he, Fabien, and his companion, were alive. Similar to those thieves of fabled cities, immured within the treasure-chambers from which there is no escape. Amid the frozen gems they wander, infinitely rich yet doomed.

17

One of the radio operators at the Comodoro Rivadavia airfield in Patagonia made a sudden gesture, and all those who had been keeping a helpless vigil with him at the base crowded hastily around. A strong light fell on the blank sheet of paper over which they craned their necks. The radio operator's hand paused in mid-air, faintly swivelling the pencil. The radio operator's hand still held the letters captive, but already the fingers twitched.

'Thunderstorms?'

The operator nodded. The static made it difficult for him to understand. Then he scrawled a few illegible letters, then words. At last they could make out the text:

'Blocked at 12,000 feet above storm. Flying due west towards interior, having drifted out to sea. No visibility below. Can't tell if still overflying the sea. Please inform if storm extends into interior.'

Because of the thunderstorms this telegram had to be relayed from base to base all the way to Buenos Aires. The message progressed through the night like a beacon, lit from watchtower to watchtower.

The reply came back from Buenos Aires: 'Storm over all interior. How much fuel have you left?'

'Half an hour.'

The words, relayed from post to post, travelled back to Buenos Aires.

In less than thirty minutes the plane was condemned to plunge into a cyclone that would drive it to its doom against a hidden reef of land.

18

Rivière was sunk in thought. He had given up all hope: this plane would founder somewhere in the night. He recalled a scene which had greatly impressed him as a child: a pond being emptied to find a body. Here too nothing would be found until this flood of darkness had been sloughed off the earth and the sands, the plains, the wheatfields had been brought back to the light. Some humble peasants might chance upon two young bodies, their elbows crooked across their faces as though asleep, scattered through the depths of the golden grass. But the night would have drowned them.

Rivière thought of the treasures buried in the depths of the night as in fabled seas . . . Night's apple trees waiting for daybreak with their as yet unfallen blossoms. The night is rich, filled with scents and sleeping lambs and still uncoloured flowers. But bit by bit the lush furrows, the moist woods, the fresh pastures will rise towards the daylight. Among the now harmless hills and prairies, and among the little lambs two children will seem to sleep, cradled in the bosom of the world. But something will have sunk from the visible world towards the other.

Rivière was familiar with the anxious tenderness of Fabien's wife, this love that had been lent her like a toy to a poor child. And Rivière thought of Fabien's hand which for a few more minutes would hold his fate in its control. This hand that had caressed, this hand that had settled on a breast and aroused a tumult in it, like a god's. This hand that had lingered on a face and changed that face. This hand which wrought miracles.

Fabien tonight was wandering over the vast splendour of a sea of clouds, but below him lay eternity. He was lost among the constellations whose only denizen he was. He still held the world in his hands and balanced it against his chest. In his wheel he gripped the weight of human riches, and from one star to the next he was desperately peddling a useless treasure he would soon be made to yield.

A radio station was still listening to him, Rivière reflected. A faint melodic beat, a modulation in the minor key was all that now linked Fabien to the world. Not a plaint, not a cry. Only the purest sound despair has ever formed.

19

Robineau roused him from his loneliness.

'Monsieur le Directeur, I've been thinking ... we could perhaps try ...'

He had nothing to propose but thus proclaimed his good intentions. He would have so liked to come up with a solution, and he still sought one worriedly, like an answer to a conundrum. He always came up with solutions which Rivière never heeded. 'In life, Robineau, there are no solutions. There are forces on the move, forces one must set in motion, and then the solutions follow.' Robineau thus limited his role to setting up a motive force in the corps of the mechanics: a humble motive force which kept the propeller-bosses from rusting.

But the events of this night were more than Robineau could cope with. His title of inspector made no impression on the storms, nor on a phantom crew which was no longer battling for a punctuality bonus but to evade that dire penalty which nullified all of Robineau's – death. Now become superfluous, Robineau wandered aimlessly through the offices.

*

Fabien's wife had herself announced. Tormented by anxiety, she waited in the secretaries' office till Rivière could receive her. The secretaries shot stealthy glances at hei face. It filled her with a kind of shame and she looked around with fright. Everything here was hostile to her. These men continuing their work as though they were trampling on a corpse, those files on which human life and suffering left no more than a residue of heartless figures. At home everything bespoke his absence: the rumpled bed, the coffee tray, a bouquet of flowers. But here . . . there was not a sign, not a token. Everything warred with pity, friendship, remembrance. The only phrase she caught – for in her presence everyone spoke in undertones – was an oath uttered by an employee who had been demanding an invoice: 'The invoice for the dynamos, for God's sake! The ones we sent to Santos.' She looked at the man with an expression of utter bewilderment, and then at the wall, covered by a map. Her lips trembled slightly, almost imperceptibly.

She realized with embarrassment that here she represented an alien truth. She almost regretted having come, would have liked to hide, and for fear of attracting too much attention, restrained herself from coughing or crying. She felt out of place, indecent, as though naked. Yet so forceful was her truth that the furtive glances kept returning, unseen, to read the expression on her face. She was a woman of unusual beauty. She was the living revelation of the sacred world of happiness. She was the living revelation of the august matter one unwittingly tampers with when one acts. Disconcerted by so many curious glances, she closed her eyes, revealing the peace one can unwittingly destroy.

Rivière received her.

She had come to make a timid plea on behalf of her flowers, her waiting coffee, her young flesh. In this office, which was even colder than the others, her lips once again began to tremble faintly. She too now discovered her own truth in this other, alien world. The almost savage, fervent, devoted quality of her love seemed to her to assume an egotistical, an importunate guise. She would have liked to flee.

'I am disturbing you . . .'

'Madame,' Rivière said to her, 'you are not disturbing me. Unfortunately, Madame, you and I can do nothing more than wait.'

There was a faint tremor in her shoulders. Rivière guessed its meaning: 'What's the point of that lamp, that waiting supper, the flowers I'll be going back to?' A young mother had one day confessed to Rivière: 'The death of my child is something I still haven't understood. It's the tiny things that are hard, his little baby clothes I keep finding, and when I wake up at night that wave of tenderness which rises in my heart, in spite of everything, and which is now so useless, like my milk . . .' For this woman too Fabien's death would not really begin until tomorrow – in each act, each object, henceforth vain. Rivière had to hide the deep pity he felt for her.

'Madame . . .'

The young woman withdrew, with an almost humble smile, unconscious of her power.

Rivière sat down heavily.

'Still, she's helped me discover what I was looking for . . .'

Absent-mindedly he fingered the weather reports which had come in from the northern airfields. 'We don't ask to be eternal,' he thought. 'What we ask is not to see acts and objects abruptly lose their meaning. The void surrounding us then suddenly yawns on every side.'

His eyes strayed back to the telegrams. 'And this is how death creeps into our affairs – through these messages, now bereft of meaning . . .'

He looked at Robineau. That middling fellow had also lost his meaning and was useless. Rivière addressed him almost gruffly:

'Must I be the one to find things for you to do?'

Rivière pushed through the door leading into the secretaries' office. He was struck by certain tell-tale signs Madame Fabien had been unable to detect. A slip marked R.B. 903 – the number of Fabien's plane – was already tacked up on the wall chart under the heading of 'Unavailable Material'. The secretaries who were preparing the clearance papers for the Europe-bound mail were working slackly, knowing that its departure would be delayed. The airfield was ringing through for instructions to give the crews who now found themselves on night duty with nothing to do. The pace of life was slowing down. 'Death, there it is!' thought Rivière. His work was now becalmed, like a stricken sailing vessel on a windless sea.

He heard Robineau's voice: 'Monsieur le Directeur . . . they'd been married just six weeks.'

'Get on with your work,' said Rivière, pulling out his watch. Looking at the secretaries, he thought of the mechanics, the groundcrews, the pilots, of all those who had helped him in his task with a faith of builders. He thought of the little ports of long ago which having heard speak of magic 'Isles', set to work to build a ship. A ship to be freighted with their hopes, whose sails would one day fill with the breath of their dreams as it headed out to sea. Thanks to a ship all of them were aggrandized, all delivered of themselves. 'The end perhaps justifies nothing, but action delivers man from death. These men lasted by virtue of their ship.'

Rivière too would be struggling against death, once he could restore full meaning to these telegrams, anxiety to the crews on duty, and a dramatic goal to his pilots. Once the breath of life revived this enterprise, as the wind revives a sail-boat on the sea.

20

Comodoro Rivadavia could now hear nothing; but twenty minutes later and six hundred miles to the north, Bahía Blanca picked up a second message:

'Beginning descent. Entering clouds . . .'

Then these two words from a blurred message were intercepted by the radio station at Trelew:

'. . . see nothing . . .'

Short-wave transmissions are like that. They are picked up in one place but elsewhere one hears nothing. Then, for no apparent reason, everything is changed. A plane, whose position is unknown, suddenly manifests itself to the world of the living, out of time and space, and the words that show up on the empty pads of radio stations are already those of phantoms.

Was the fuel supply exhausted, or was the pilot playing his last card before his engine failed – trying to make contact with the ground without crashing?

'Put the question to him,' Buenos Aires ordered Trelew.

*

The radio station looks a bit like a laboratory – with its nickel and copper strips, its tuners and its sheaves of wires. In their white overalls the radio operators seem silently bent over a simple experiment. With their delicate fingers they manipulate the instruments, explore the magnetic sky, diviners probing for the vein of gold.

'No answer?'

'No answer.'

Perhaps they will catch this note which would be a sign of life. If the plane and its wing-lights rise up among the stars, they may perhaps head the song of this errant star.

The seconds ooze by. They really ooze like blood. Are they still in the air, or is their flight ended? Each second slays a hope. The flow of time now seems destructive. Twenty centuries of wear and tear, beating against the temple, nibbling and fissuring the granite and finally reducing it to dust, are now concentrated into each second threatening the crew.

Each second carries something away – Fabien's voice, Fabien's laugh, his smile. The silence gains ground. A heavier and heavier silence, bearing down on his crew like the weight of the sea.

'It's 1.40,' someone finally observes. 'The extreme limit of their fuel. They can't be flying any more.'

Now all is calm. The watchers are left with a bitter taste in the mouth, like that of a journey's end. Something mysterious has come to pass, something a bit sickening. In the midst of all these nickelled plates and copper arteries one experiences the gloom that reigns over ruined factories. All this material seems ponderous, useless, unemployed, a weight of dead branches.

One can only wait for daylight.

In a few hours all of Argentina will emerge into the daylight, and these men will be there still, like fishermen on the strand, watching the net that is being slowly, oh so slowly dragged in, and without their knowing what it will contain.

*

In his office Rivière now felt the *détente* which comes in the aftermath of great disasters, when man is released from fate's uncertainty. He had alerted the police of an entire province. He could do no more, he could only wait. But order must reign even in the house of the dead.

Rivière beckoned to Robineau:

'Get this message off to the northern airfields: "Anticipate serious delay Patagonia mail-plane. To avoid undue delay Europe mail, will add Patagonia to next Europe mail."

Feeling a jab of pain, he bent forward a little. Then, with an effort, he remembered something, something serious. Ah yes! Lest he forget it he called: 'Robineau!'

'Monsieur Rivière?'

'You will draft a memo. Pilots are forbidden to exceed 1,900 r.p.m. They're wrecking the engines.'

'Very well, Monsieur Rivière.'

Rivière bowed his head, a little further. Solitude, above all, was what he needed.

'That's all, Robineau. You can run along, old man . . .'

And Robineau felt almost frightened at this equality before the dark unknown.

21

Robineau now wandered sadly through the offices. The life of the Company was at a standstill; for the Europe-bound mail, due to leave at 2 a.m., would now not leave before dawn. The employees sat morosely by their desks, frozen-faced now that their vigil was pointless. From the northern airfields the weather reports kept coming in at a steady pace; but their 'clear skies', 'full moon', and 'no wind' evoked the image of a lifeless kingdom. A desert of moonlight and stones.

As Robineau, for no particular reason, began leafing through a file the head clerk had been working on, he suddenly realized that the latter was standing in front of him, waiting with an air of mocking deference to get it back. The expression on his face seemed to say: 'When it pleases you, you know . . . It's mine . . .'

The inspector felt shocked by this attitude on the part of a subordinate, but unable to think of a retort, he handed the file brusquely back. The head clerk resumed his seat with an air of grave superiority. 'I should have sent him packing,' thought Robineau. To regain face he walked on, his thoughts focused on the crisis. This crisis would entail the abandonment of a policy, and Robineau felt a sense of twofold loss.

He was assailed by the vision of Rivière, alone there in his office, Rivière who had said to him '. . . old man'. Never had someone so lacked support as he. Robineau felt a floodtide of compassion go out towards him. In his mind he turned over a number of phrases vaguely aimed to express sympathy and consolation. He was moved by a feeling which struck him as quite noble.

He now knocked gently on the door. There was no answer. Not daring to knock more loudly in the prevailing silence, he pushed open the door. Rivière was there. For the first time Robineau entered Rivière's office almost on an equal footing, a bit like a friend. He felt a bit like the sergeant who joins the wounded general under fire, stands by him in defeat, and behaves like a brother to him in exile. 'Whatever happens, I am with you,' Robineau seemed to say.

Rivière spoke not a word; his head somewhat bowed, he was looking at his hands. Robineau, standing before him, dared not speak. Even stricken, the old lion daunted him. Expressions of loyalty, of ever more rapt devotion kept mounting to his lips, but each time he raised his eyes he encountered the grey hair, the head three-quarters bowed, the lips tight-sealed over their bitter potion. Finally he screwed up his courage:

'Monsieur le Directeur . . .'

Rivière raised his head and looked at him. The reverie into

which Rivière had been plunged was so deep, so distant that he may not yet have noticed Robineau's presence. Nor could anyone know what it was he had been dreaming, feeling, and mourning in his heart. Rivière looked at Robineau for a long instant as a living witness to something. Robineau felt ill at ease. The longer Rivière looked at Robineau, the more it seemed as if a smile of enigmatic irony was playing about the former's lips. The longer Rivière looked at Robineau, the deeper Robineau blushed and the more it seemed to Rivière that Robineau had come, with a touching and regrettably spontaneous goodwill, to bear witness to the foolishness of human beings.

Robineau felt increasingly dismayed. The sergeant, the general, the bullets all now seemed grotesquely out of place. A puzzling transformation came over him. Rivière was still looking at him. Robineau, almost despite himself, straightened up a bit and took his hand out of his left pocket. Rivière still looked at him. Whereupon, feeling an intense embarrassment and not quite knowing why, Robineau blurted out:

'I have come to receive your orders.'

Rivière pulled out his watch and said in the simplest of tones:

'It's 2 o'clock. The mail-plane from Asunción will land at 2.10. Have the Europe-bound mail-plane take off at 2.15.'

Robineau went out to propagate the astounding news: the night flights were not being interrupted.

'Bring me that file of yours to check,' said Robineau to the chief clerk.

'Wait!' he said when the chief clerk was in front of him.

And the chief clerk waited.

22

The mail-plane from Asunción signalled that it was about to land. Even during the most critical moments Rivière had followed its successful progress telegram by telegram. In the midst of the débâcle this was his revenge, the living proof of his faith. This successful flight augured a thousand others that would be equally successful. 'We don't get a cyclone every night,' thought Rivière. 'And once the trail is blazed, there is nothing for it but to continue.'

Descending, airfield by airfield, from Paraguay, as though from an enchanted garden filled with flowers, pavilions, and slow waters, the plane had skirted the edge of a cyclone which had failed to dim a single star. Wrapped in their travelling rugs, the nine passengers pressed their foreheads to the panes, as though before a shop window full of gems: already the towns of Argentina were stringing their gold beads across the night, beneath the paler gold of the cities of stars above. Up front the pilot held his precious cargo of human lives in his hands, his wide-open eyes filled with moonlight, like a goatherd. The horizon already glowed with the rosy fire of Buenos Aires, and soon, like a fabled treasure, it would flaunt its diadem of jewels. The radio operator was tapping out the final telegrams, like the last notes of a sonata gaily tinkled in the sky for Rivière's enjoyment. Then he pulled in the aerial, stretched himself a bit, yawned, and smiled. The trip was over.

The pilot, after landing, found the pilot of the Europe-bound mail leaning against his plane with his hands in his pockets.

'You're flying the next hop?'

'Yes.'

'Is the Patagonia in?'

'We're not waiting for it. It's disappeared. Good weather?'

'Weather's fine. You mean Fabien's disappeared?'

They said little; for a deep sense of brotherhood made extra phrases unnecessary.

While the mailbags from Asunción were being transferred to the Europe-bound plane, the pilot, leaning back against the fuselage, stood there motionless, gazing up at the stars. He felt a mighty power stirring within him, and it filled him with a potent joy.

'All loaded?' a voice asked. 'O.K. Contact!'

The pilot did not budge, as his engine was started. Leaning back against the plane with his shoulders, he could feel the plane begin to live. Now at last, after so many false alarms – will leave ... won't leave ... will leave – the pilot would know for sure. His lips parted and his teeth glistened under the moon like a lion cub's.

'Watch out! The night, eh ...'

He didn't hear his companion's advice. His hands in his pockets, his head thrown back, he thought of the clouds and the mountains, the rivers and the seas, and he broke into a silent laugh. A faint laugh which ran through him, like a breeze through a tree, and which thrilled him to the core. A faint laugh, but so much stronger than those clouds and mountains, those seas and rivers.

'Say, what's tickling you?'

'That fool Rivière who told me ... who seems to think I'm scared!'

23

In a minute he would be flying over Buenos Aires, and Rivière, who had resumed the struggle, wanted to hear him. Hear him murmur, roar, and die away, like the mighty tramp of an army marching through the stars.

His arms folded, Rivière passed among his secretaries. He paused behind a window and listened thoughtfully. If he had held up even one departure, his battle on behalf of night flights would have been lost. But to forestall the craven-hearted who tomorrow would disown him, Rivière had launched this other crew into the night.

Victory ... defeat ... these words are meaningless. Life lies deeper than these images, and is already at work, preparing new ones. A victory weakens one nation, defeat arouses another. The defeat Rivière had suffered was perhaps the commitment needed to spur on the decisive victory. For what mattered was the onward movement, the momentum.

In five minutes the radio stations would have alerted the airfields, and over ten thousand miles the quickening pulse of life would be resolving all problems.

Already a deep organ note was swelling – the plane.

And Rivière returned to his work, walking slowly past the secretaries cowed by his stern gaze. Rivière the Great, Rivière the Triumphant, bearing his heavy burden of victory.